Nicholas Flood Davin

Eos : An Epic of the Dawn

And other Poems

Nicholas Flood Davin

Eos : An Epic of the Dawn
And other Poems

ISBN/EAN: 9783337206932

Printed in Europe, USA, Canada, Australia, Japan

Cover: Foto ©Andreas Hilbeck / pixelio.de

More available books at **www.hansebooks.com**

EOS:

AN EPIC OF THE DAWN.

AND OTHER POEMS.

BY

NICHOLAS FLOOD DAVIN. M.P.

REGINA, N.W.T.
LEADER COMPANY (LIMITED.)
MDCCCLXXXIX.

CONTENTS

PREFACE.

ERRATA.

p. iv. in 6th line—Hygeia for Hygie.

p. 112—Hygeia for Hygiea.

line 7 ! for ?

" 8 ! ." ?

imagination as important as the raising of grain. The raising
of grain will bring us wealth, but intellectual progress, on
which again the highest development of our material resources depends, will be slow unless all the faculties of the
mind are stimulated. The greatest merchants the world ever
saw were highly cultivated men, great and discriminating
patrons of literature, with not merely a keen eye to the
profit of a commercial transaction, but a quick and true sense

PREFACE.

The following attempts were written from time to time as impulse prompted. "I lisped in numbers for the numbers came," such as they were. But soon after I began to earn my bread, I arrived at the conclusion that with the cream skimmed off the mind by newspaper writing, and engaged in the exacting study of law, I could not, even if I had the native gift, hope to write poetry which should be at once original and of high workmanship. The terror of

Medioeribus esse poetis
Non homines, non dii, non concessere Columnae,

was on me; and save one work which was well advanced, but which now may never see the light, the tragedies, comedies, idylls, epics I contemplated, died unborn.

Why then do I publish these things? I am probably not so vain as I was in my twenty-third year. I have learned to be afraid of nothing but God and wrong-doing, and hold it cowardice to shrink from endeavour thro' fear of failure. I am a North-West man, and I think the cultivation of taste and imagination as important as the raising of grain. The raising of grain will bring us wealth, but intellectual progress, on which again the highest development of our material resources depends, will be slow unless all the faculties of the mind are stimulated. The greatest merchants the world ever saw were highly cultivated men, great and discriminating patrons of literature, with not merely a keen eye to the profit of a commercial transaction, but a quick and true sense of literary excellence; and I rejoice to know we have on many of our farms educated men, and that the Saskatchewan can boast of a successful merchant who has won a high place in the ranks of Canadian poets.

We need in Canada generally a broader intellectual air; redemption from the domination of sciolists, with hearts often as contracted as their culture; the consciousness that we have within ourselves all that can make a great people; and every step towards the creation of a Canadian literature tends to hasten the new and better era in whose advent I believe. The late Mr. Arnold denounced the English Philistine; the Philistine is not the pest we have to complain of. Wherever we turn we are met by people without respect for decency or truth. The Philistine of Arnold is a man with inherited ideas, dominated by prejudice and intolerant of enlightenment. But while thankful for brilliant and instructed publicists, we cannot deny that we have gorillas who presume to instruct mankind on every subject, and express what they call public opinion, whose teaching is degrading, and the weapons of whose warfare are calumny and lies.

Again, before a great poet can arise there must be a large number of writers to prepare, not merely the mind of the nation for him, but to accumulate material on which his more plastic hand shall work. The extraordinary versatility of Shakespeare, his command of every note in the human soul, — this is not due to his genius alone; it is due, in great part, to the fact that he absorbed, adopted, exploited the works of other men, many of whom thought and wrote amid conditions wholly different from those of his own country and time.

A great critic has pronounced the main idea of Eos "undeniably happy." One not less competent wrote me it was "original and happy," and regretted I had not made all that could be made of it. I have endeavoured to do more justice to the opportunities it presents, but I know well how much more might have been done; and perhaps hereafter a cunninger hand, and one more favourably circumstanced, will take it up and sing a song worthier than mine. Even then, though my little star will be lost in the blaze of his, I shall have done something in my humble way for literature.

These verses came as the fly stung, or as I was urged by friends, (some of whom might have stood up rivals to the Muses), to write, with an exception in the case of the second edition of Eos, as now published, and another work already referred to, written before I had grown to manhood.

While wandering about London and Paris in 1887, I wrote the verses to "The Critics." I had intended publishing what now appears and something more in London, but the readers of the publishing houses were away holiday making, and I had not time to await their return. Some of the smaller pieces are purely imaginary; some were written in very early life.

The first edition of "Eos" had the distinction of being dedicated to Lady Macdonald. I here recall the fact that I may put on record the regard I bear a great and good woman, and express my gratitude to her for her ennobling influence. To know her is to be a better man. While writing "The Critics" a dedication of this volume was made impulsively, and not unnaturally, to another lady, not so great, but not less, by reason of every womanly virtue, an honour to her sex.

This is the first purely literary work printed and published in the North-West Territories. Let us hope it is the small beginning of great things. It is the product of stray moments in a busy, and, for some twelve years, a turbulent life.

I have in "The Critics" dealt with those criticisms on "Eos" which were capable of being treated in verse. With regard to such criticisms as that I ended some of the lines with a preposition, all I have to say is I do not agree with the view that this is always a fault. Milton, Byron, and other great masters, frequently close a line with a preposition. I am inclined to think in the present day the poet is lost in the artist, and that we need a reaction analagous to that which Cowper unconsciously led against the imitators of

Pope. Where I could, I have bowed to my judges. I have
even changed the title to please those who objected to my
calling it "a prairie dream." I may say, however, the de-
scription of the home of Eos was composed in sleep, and when
I awoke I wrote it down. This suggested the poem.

The descriptions of Paris and London in this edition of
Eos are founded on careful observation. I saw the sun rise
over Paris from the Arc de Triomphe. In order to correct
and guide the imagination, I read the accounts of their im-
pressions published by balloonists. "Eos" is, I hope, now
less open to the charge of want of balance and proportion.

Many men engaged in active life as I am, would shrink in
our community from publishing verses; but to my thinking,
it is a duty to educate the people out of the narrow, not to
say brutal view, that a man must be a mere specialist. In
all times, and all countries, the highest ability for practical
affairs has been conjoined with versatility, and a Canadian
politician need not fear an ignorant sneer which could have
been flung at a statesman like Canning.

I will probably never write another verse. Despairing of
leisure in the future, I throw these on the stream with all
their imperfections—and as, while the book was passing
through the press, I was hurried from one end to the other of
a vast constituency—the defects, in mechanical workmanship
alone, cannot be few or far between. Let them sink or swim.
If they sink, they will find themselves in very good company;
and if they swim a little day, it is about as much as most
modern works can hope for.

REGINA, Jan. 21st, 1889.

My Mother! o'er wide leagues of land,
  And over belts of roaring brine,
I reach thee this unworthy hand,
  And strain to touch these lips with thine.

For as when day's bright glare is o'er,
  And stealing shadows longer drawn,
The moments, sad and swift, restore
  Effects like those of early dawn :

And as the Autumn storms tear
  The whirling leaves from swaying boughs,
Revealing, mid the branches bare,
  Some nest where birds were used to house;

So, as life's shadows longer grow,
  And passion's power and dreams of youth
Decline, the child's heart's outlines show
  Amid the bare bleak boughs of truth :

And tho' that heart be well nigh dead,
  And never more new joys can thrill,
Its every fluttering impulse fled,
  Its build is as you made it still :

Still strong with bonds of home-knit love,
  And your own will, which did not quail
Amid all trouble, high above
  What's mean, it rocks in life's wild gale

The cloudlet's frown that did deface
  Our strong love's all-embracing joy—
Long past—has left behind no trace :
  I love you now as when a boy :

And blend with this small book your name,
  Which breathes of babblings round your knee—
Whereat you smiled, half-posed——of fame,
  Great deeds, glad flights o'er land and sea :

And therein songs you'll lightly scan,
  Wherein my heart for love was fain :
They show me weak : they prove me man :
  They're bursts of joy, or births of pain.

Thanks, gentlemen, for your fair criticisms,
    Which, to be frank, I think were far too kind ;
I also thank you for your witticisms,
    Which showed your kindness did not 'go it blind.'
Tho' some remarks proved there were little schisms
    Within your ranks, I think that here you'll find
I've tried to profit by most things you taught me.
The only profit the edition brought me.

I will say this, it pleased me much to see
    The rancour that in other paths pursue
My steps, did not contaminate the free
    And open air of literature, and you
My generous foes who did for once agree
    To see some merit, and to say so too,
In what I did, I thank you from my heart,
Ah ! if we'd all at all times play that part !

I take my inspiration from a muse,
    Whose dainty feet ne'er trod the hill Parnassus,
Yet if you saw her, you would not refuse
    To own her sway, for sweeter than molasses
Is her soft smile serene; nor could you choose,
    Unless indeed quite crazy, or as crass as
A fool, but own that of the Nine as any
She's as fair, or were there twice as many.

Therefore perhaps, my flight though with a goddess,
   May not have soar'd so high as 'twould have run.
If my inspirer didn't wear a bodice,
   Likewise a bustle when her toilet's done.
But then a glance — you would not think it odd is
   That for no undraped maid that ever won
Apollo's smile I'd change.   Inured to rustlin'
In our North-West — I like a muse in muslin,

Or silk, or crape, or calico;   I ask
   But this that it be cut and stitched with skill,
Nor outlines mar in which the eye would bask,
   Whose beauty heart and mind and soul can fill
With joy.   It should not be too hard a task
   To drape sweet nature's handiwork, and still
Preserve the entrancing grace of God's *chef d'œuvre*
As did the Greeks of old: go see the Louvre.

Think you we'd pause before each statue there,
   O'er which the flowing marble's drapery falls,
If this concealed the lines of beauty rare,
   The stately loveliness which soul enthralls,
Perfection's essence, now beyond compare ?
   Ye who obey the monthly fashion's calls,
Here might ye learn how grace may be disgraced
By camel humps and corsets tightly laced.

But fashion's ugliness can uglier be
   If skilless artists make the lady's dress,
Therefore fair reader, look to it and see
   That yours shall deftly every point express.

Save what the moment's hideous fantasy
    Insists on hiding.   But e'en then I guess
Good taste deformity can minimize,
And sun-like beauty breaks thro' all disguise.

Yet never think you need not reck the style :
    'Tis true no milliner can dim your eye,
Or sour the sweetness of your honied smile,
    Or steal its peril from your bosom's sigh,
Or cover o'er a solitary wile ;
    But as saltpetre makes the dwarf as high
As Anak's sons, so fashion's ceaseless whirls
Tend to equality among the girls.

This muse of mine in no way analytical,
    Of mind constructive, leans to synthesis,
Therefore it is not that I would be critical,
    But as in postscript or parenthesis,
We mention something private or political,
    We'd like to note without much emphasis,
On one or two remarks I would remark,
If but to show I wrote not in the dark.

One critic said 'twas wrong to make a pause
    In the swift goddess's transorbic run,
Because 'twas contrary to nature's laws,
    And she'd be surely caught up by the sun.
With due respect he hardly weigh'd the cause,
    Nor thought of what for Joshua he'd done.
If once to please a man a long pause made he,
He'd make a short one just to please a lady.

Another pointed out that Eos could not sleep,
   Eternal wakefulness her doom decreed;
Another said 'twas wrong to make her weep;
   Another that he knew she could not read;
Then how he ask'd in politics be deep,
   And pose as if the world she meant to lead
In wiser ways ? To all this I reply :
The thing's a dream— I dreamt I saw her cry,

That fast as dove with head beneath her wing
   I saw her sleep, though her all glorious head
Was not conceal'd, but radiant shone, a thing
   For Millais at his best to paint. Of red
A touch to her dishevelled gold he'd bring,
   Nor spoil the beauty poor Tithonus wed.
But tho' of carrotty tones he is so fond,
I'd rather see him paint her perfect blonde.

Then if no leisure hour the goddess claimed
   When had she time to woo ? But yet we know
There's hardly one in all the skies so famed
   For captivating fairest men below.
The stricture about reading too lies maimed,
   For heavenly minds with intuition glow.
In days when all we mortals know our letters,
Pray can we limit our immortal betters ?

Why she talk'd politics, I cannot say,
   Perhaps in heaven they take the *Daily News*,
And *Telegraph*, and *Times*, and duly lay
   To heart the lessons which these sheets infuse.

I'm sure they take the *Sun* and so they may
   Know all the babble of the mart and mews,
Take *Truth* and *Bell's Life* and thus to sport
Add all the gossip of our brilliant court.

The *Pall Mall* certes finds an entrance there,
   And boys with wings distribute weekly papers,
The *Saturday, Spectator* and the *Fair*,
   The *World* where Edmund cuts his weekly capers,
All these and more to make the seraphs stare,
   With fashion prints from milliners and drapers,
Are taken in and conn'd by heavenly eyes,
And mortal's deeds immortals much surprise.

Most certainly they've read I cannot say 'poor *devils*,'
   All the descriptions of the jubilee,
Of royal dinners and of royal revels,
   Of our fine fleet upon our silver sea,
Of cutlasses and bayonets in shrivels ;
   I hope they'll never see what ne'er should be,
Our fine fleet batter'd like a piece of crockery,
And all our glory 'monumental mockery.'

How brought she then no horse-race on the tapis ?
   Why told she not of dinners and of balls ?
Of scandals not yet cold but sweet and sappy ?
   Of paltry rivalries in royal halls ?
Of princes drest in suits of warlike nappy,
   Who'd be quite lost to meet their duties' calls ?
Her views on politics might be exprest
Because she thought I'd like the subject best.

The dream's dramatic, tho' by no strict rules
   My muse who wears a smock, evolves her story;
"Out west," you know we're rebels to old schools,
   And in our independence rather glory,
For this I hope you'll here not dub us fools,
   And as on strict condition that no more he
'd err, at times, a culprit gets off free,
Against harsh judgment I might make a plea.

But no! if I've presumed too fond and far,
   Lay on the lash and make me rue the deed;
In other walks I've heard and felt the jar
   Of bitter conflict, but I did not bleed
Quite unavenged, nor weakly doubt my star.
   But here, in unaccustomed fields, a reed
I'll bow to whatsoever comes. The blow
Will only tell me what I fully know,

That art requires not only high vocation,
   But all life's vows and hours laid on her shrine,
Too deep I've drunk th' unspeakable elation
   Of Shakespeare's song and 'Marlowe's mighty line,'
And Milton's epic, Dante (in translation),
   Old Homer, Horace, Virgil, and in fine
I've march'd with all the singers of the world,
Their banners to eternity unfurled

Above me all unworthy; but I felt
   The rythmic clangour of their sonorous songs
All beauty, greatness breathing, and I knelt
   In heart and worshipp'd, learning there all wrongs

To hate and war on, tho' hot hell should pelt,
   And low corruption sound her myriad gongs,
To call her minions 'gainst whoever stands
For right and light, in free or fetter'd lands.

Therefore I know this little song of mine
   For what it is ; my highest hope that here
I've struck a warning note, pointed a line
   Of action that may ward off what I fear
For England, Ireland, Empire. These should shine
   Twin island stars of power and peace ; too near
For aught but love. Now love is for the free
In equal fortunes and strict equity.

I also wished—too daring or too vain !
   To strike from greater anvils still a spark,
To guide some groper o'er the trailless plain,
   And show him where to wend tho' all be dark.
For honest hearts a faith that's not inane
   But full of comfort, calls men to an ark,
Will safely ride the troubled waves of life,
And give them peace amid its stormy strife,

Tho' the loud thunder bellow's o'er the tide
   Submerging all our hopes and all we love,
And wailing winds, like spirits that deride
   Joy, trust, and truth, howl round and from above,
Whence light should shower, the wild wrack spreads its
      wide
   Horizon-touching wings, yet comes this dove
Hope's branch held in its beak, whose green leaves tell
God's forces rule and all for all is well.

And doing this, this far-west flower of verse,
    May stir a heart or two with beauty seen
By me but never ha'f expressed, the curse
    Of long immersion in the world's din
Being on me, and my cruel fate far worse
    Than those who strive but fail the prize to win,
For they sketch o'er the course and all but touch
The goal, while I—my Pegasus a crutch !

A foolish boy, alas ! long summers since,
    I cast my horoscope for highest things,
And thought by strength the world I should convince,
    And that with time I'd feel my budding wings.
I said : ' I'll take my cue from every prince
    Of song ; from every harp its sweetest strings ;'
And fancy walked thro' all the muse's maze,
Thro' all song's avenues and haunted ways.

And then I wrote presumptuous : ' I will climb
    And write in starry characters my name
Where the great blaze of Byron's song sublime
    Makes the lame bard the cynosure of fame ;'
And all I asked from heaven was health and time
    Doubt's craven fears and envy's sneers to shame,
When up stalked Poverty and wrought me ill,
And fiery passions fought the fiery will.

Here's but an echo of a song that wanes,
    Thrown from far studies and forgotten years,
Like sounds of anthems in deserted fanes,
    Hymns' phantoms in the temple which uprears

Its crumbling roof and arches to the rains
   And winds, hallowed by bygone prayers and tears;
Hark to those strains! aloft and down the aisles
Reverberate! Is't only Fancy's wiles?

To thee fair spirit! of whom half in jest
   I've sung above, I dedicate to thee
These songs ; to thee, the beautiful, the best !
   My never-absent-one where'er I be !
My calm mid scenes where howling winds infest,
   And where peace blooms the fairest flower for me,
Far, far—yet near--I send across the sea
These songs to thee, my beautiful, to thee !

LONDON, August, 1887.

EOS: AN EPIC OF THE DAWN.

Illusion makes the better part of life.
Happy self-conjurors, deceived, we win
Delight and ruled by fancy live in dreams.
The mood, the hour, the standpoint, rules the scene ;
The past, the present, the to-be weave charms ;
White-flashing memory's fleet footsteps fly,
And all the borders of her way are pied
With flowers full glad e'en when their roots touch quick
With pain.   With tears upon his dimpled cheek
Forth steps the infant joy, and laughing, mocks
At care.   In time, smiles play upon the cheek
Of pale regret, who grows transformed, and stands
A pensive queen, more fair than boisterous mirth.
The present's odorous with leaves of trees
Long dead, and dead defacing weeds and thorns,
And past the cloud that glowered, the blast that smote,
And out from never to be trodden days
Hope smiles, and airs from dawns we're never doomed
To see, come rich with fragrance, fresh with power,
Profuse of promises of golden days,
And join the necromancy of the past,
Mingling the magic which makes up our lives.

I had been musing how the goddess bright
Of morning red, at close of every night,
Announcing coming light of day to gods

And mortals, drove her lambent car across
The sky, and how she stoop'd and pluck'd those flowers
Of men, —Orion, Cephalus, Tithonus —
Tithonus, who became a wrinkled shade,
So changed from him whose strength and beauty pierced
The heart of Eos in its tender dawn
Of love.

      A sunny sky of blue arching
A plain in verdure drowned, and floating thick
Upon the emerald sea sweet wild flowers gay ;
Their stately queen the light-pink prairie rose.
The whirr of insects loud on every side,
And loud and clear the prairie lark, deep hid
In those vast fragrant meadows, sang ; the creek
Sent thousand-voiced upon the sultry air
The bull-frog's weary canticle. I slept
And dreamt the goddess bent above me there
On that wide treeless plain, and made my heart
Distend with dumb, bewildering, dreadful joy ;
Near mine the snowy forehead isled in gold,
Near mine the eyes of blue, ineffable, sweet,
And on my mouth the dewy rose of hers.
She rose and bared her milk-white arm, and drew
Me near her ; then there flash'd a blinding light ;
Whirlwinds of flame swept o'er the grass ; the plain
Was one vast fire from rim to rim ; but on
We went till distance made th' abounding blaze
Like glow of western clouds presaging storm,
When the broad sun in awful glory sets,
Then leaves great yellow fire-lit tracts behind,
Like fame of some portentous deed ; the heart

Is touched and no unpleasing sadness wraps
The soul.

       The sea soon lay beneath, with isles
Of vines and palms, tall cedars, citron groves,
Within an azure concave rimmed with light.
A rush of green-white wave and we were whelm'd
In depths wherein whole navies might go down,
Nor leave a ripple on the placid sea.
Careless, I closed mine eyes to die, but she
Reached forth the delicate hand with tapering fingers.
White, rosy-tipp'd, and touched me.   At that touch
Strength came.   I seemed to breathe my native air,
And she led on towards stately towers unique
In architecture and in ornament.
But when we neared the carven arch and door
She turned and said : —" To-morrow you shall ride
With me," and like a dream she went, and blank
And desolate, I knew not where to turn.

Far down where never sailors' plummet reach'd,
Nor ever beam of piercing sunbeam stole,
Nor dream of faint forgotten sound e'er stirred,
Nor ghost of earthly odours smote the sense,
Wall'd in with silent, fearful waves, its roof
Of night and pallid waning stars, upheld
By massy pillars quarried from the dark,
The home mysterious of the goddess stands ;
Its solemn spacious chambers carpeted
With dusk, and hung with swarthy tapestries ;
Ebon the garniture ; profuse on lounge
And litter lay the furs of animals

Extinct for centuries ere man emerged,
Of which the rocks no hint to science give.
Along the halls and corridors obscure,
In many a dim recess, rose stately shapes
Of blackness.   Fed from odorous flowers fresh culled
In gardens of Persephoné, the air
Was sweet -- a rich pervading fragrance pure,
And through the rayless splendours of these halls--
Led by what happy chance or gracious guide --
I groped and found where far within, in such
A room, so full of sleep-compelling airs,
So beautiful, so stately-solemn, still,
As silence, weary of time's fret and change
Might choose for an eternal sleep, lo ! there
On couch dark as a piece of Erebus,
But soft as Summer cloud, canning the frame,
Made from the lethal bronze the Titan works
In thunder clouds, in dreamless slumber Eos
Lay.   Ah ! no darkness there !   From white lithe limbs,
Full throat, carved shoulder, pure firm breast and waist
Which rose in beauty to the swelling hips,
Light shone, and glory from her golden head !
Athwart those hips a vaporous veil, dim lace
Of magic woof, the work of hands divine
And made from mists of dawn was thrown, but fail'd
To hide large outlines fair, which dazzling glow'd
As glows the sun thro' half-enkindled clouds.
Like small snow mounds o'er which in threshing time
The farmer spills the yellow grain, which curves
Around the base, her eyelids white ; her mouth,
Her ruddy cheeks glow'd like young roses red

Above the lilies of her throat and breast.
Around, light, airy, fairy forms kept watch.
She moved and these took wing. She rose and stood
A vision fairer than e'er sculptor dream'd,
And like a cataract of fire and gold
That down white rocks of Parian marble sweeps,
O'er shoulder, breast and flank her thick hair fell
And reached her pearly ankles pale. Her maids
Who seem'd compact of starlight, now return'd,
The bath prepared, and like to Artemis
When by the hunter spied, but riper-warm
Her beauty, Titian's to Correggio's
Venus, or what the matron of some years
Of happy married life is to the girl
She was before love struck the fountains deep
Of life and all the streams of tenderness
Set free, Eos stood while they poured the water
O'er her, parting the hair to let the wave
Reach the white back and lave the fruitful breast.
Upon her flesh the drops enamour'd stood,
Trembled and rolled unwilling down ; around
Her form a purple robe, diaphanous,
She flung, and passed into the hall where-through
Now gleam'd a light, clear, soft, diffused. Her face
Was full of youth and purpose, and she cast
No glance at all aside, nor did she heed
The helpless pathos of those filmy hands
Tithonous held out pleading, nor dumb prayers
Regard. Before the high arched carven door
There rushed the blaze of golden car and steeds
Of fire, with lightning shod, their eyes like pits

Of flame, and standing near, with harp in hand,
Spirits of beauty sang clear voiced and sweet :

CHORUS.

Hail ! day's herald reappearing !
  Joy of earth ! young earth's adorning,
Wings out-spread and fast careering
  Down the gulfs of Chaos darkling,
    Soon Black Night will disappear ;
  While her star above her sparkling,
Comes with shining robes the Morning,
    Orange-tinted, purple-glowing,
    Samite skirts and freely flowing,
    Songs of birds, and saucy crowing
    Shrill of wakeful chanticleer.

Bounding rills down bowery highlands,
  Flashing streams with streamlets flushing,
Lucid waves round flowery islands,
  In thy beams will soon be blushing,
And the lily's pallid cheek will burn with thy dyes
  And the leaves and fields will twinkle
  With the dews thy tears besprinkle,
    Tears from thine immortal eyes.

Where now darkness grimly gloometh,
  Soon leaf shadows will be swaying,
Over sunny banks where bloometh,
    Drinking draughts of sunny air,
    Sweet as love and glad as day,

Flowers too bright to know decaying,
     They are so immortal fair,'
     Though their doom be to decay.

SEMICHORUS I.

     Mount thy car !
     We come from far —
Come from watching fairies footing
   Steps fantastic in the moonlight,
     O'er enchanted lawns of green ;
On the left white billows shooting,
   Whose spray showers of margarite
     Play o'er sheets of silver sheen :
On the right a cedarn cover,
Where coy Dian with her lover
     Might have met and kissed unseen.
      Mount thy car !
     Fain would we be viewing
Thy soft tears the earth bedewing,
   The meadows green and mountains,
   The forest thick and fells,
   Leafy dells, gardened closes,
   Roses red, pink and pale,
Towery hyacinth and jasmine and blue bells,
And ten thousand flowers unnamed which regale
   With the colours they exhale.
Drunk enraptured sense subduing
   Through the perfume laden gale,
Bearing spoils from large wild roses,
From pied pansies, nectar'd posies—

Purple chalices and golden,
Of man's eyes still unbeholden,
Which the bee to-day shall drain ;
From tall grasses big with sun and rain,
From glad vines no careful hand shall train
Which run riot round wild fountains
That go flashing down the dale.

SEMICHORUS II.

Mount thy car !
Jewelled, golden, asbestine,
We would have divine delight,
And would gaze
On the maze
Of commingling waters' blaze,
On wild teeming ocean's daughters,
Lakes and seas ;
On the haze
Over lakes and wooded mountains,
Over fields and spray-crowned fountains,
Where the earliest day-gleams shiver,
On mild-glinting rill and river,
Where the youngest morning beams
Plash in streamlets play on streams,
Waterfalls, like ruby wine,
In thy amethystine light.
Mount thy car !

Now while they sang we mounted that high car,
And, ere I was aware, Eos, the reins

Held in both hands, was flying up the steep
Way phosphorescent, I beside her.   Tongues
Of flame played in the horses' manes and all
Seem'd hurrying flame, and soon the cold raw air
Of the dark world was stirred, and the stars blinked
And glimmered pale and went.   But Lucifer
In untam'd splendour shone, and up the heavens
And o'er the broad Ægean blood-red shafts
Were mixed with yellow, sapphire and beryl rays.

We saw the isles dispersed within what seemed
The hollow sea, like leaves within the cup,
When old tea-drinking crones their fortunes tell.
Afar lay Cypress whence Phœnicians came
With wares to Argos and Mycenæ, bent
On trade and plunder, stealing youth and maid
And wife with golden tresses, limbs like light,
To sell in Egypt.   On these shores they found
The shell-fish which contained their Tyrian dye.
They settled in the land, built cities long
Renown'd in song, grew rich and great, and lost
The memory of their Eastern lands less fair.
They taught the Greek their arts, their alphabet ;
To measure, mould, carve, gild, inlay,
Design ; to write in symbols and to frame
Grotesque impossible embodiments,
But Greece her own bright genius felt and soar'd
Into ideal worlds, and gave men forms
And faiths such as Divinity itself
Might charm ; the beautiful she first revealed,
And when from sleep and slaughter Europe woke

'Twas at the kiss of Greece upon her brow,
Blood-stained   the crown of grace in Plato's speech,
The majesty of Pheidian art, above
Life's lusts, and wars loud varnish, glory called—
The worship of Euripides for worth
In man and tender woman's selfless love.

Right over Athens she drew up her team,
Air-pawing, breathing blaze-mixed smoke, and down
On tower and temple, mighty ruins, grey
Old columns of past empire, glory showered.
A buried world rose up before mine eye.
Methought to greet us, awful Pallas came,
Cold, love proof maid, serene, omnipotent
In arms, who never snatch'd from human fields
A mortal youth, to dare the perils dread
Of charms divine, nor ever shed a tear,
No, not when battlefields were heaped with slain,
And widows tore their hair and screamed, and wild
With woe-compelling grief, the lonely couch
A river made ; her followed, glorious throng,
The singers, statesmen, sages, heroes old,
All that made Athens glory's shrine, the world's
Pharos ; while far from Thebes Memnonian strains
Were borne thro' many a flowery-scented vale.
The mind of Eos turned to him she bore
Tithonus, his ripe beauty and his fate
Unripe, by fierce Achilles sent to death.
Her large blue orbs were dimmed with tears, such tears
As weep immortal eyes, and swift, all blades
Of grass, all leaves, all flowers were gemm'd with dew :

And oh ! her beauty as she swept away
Those drops from cheeks fit thrones for love and joy !
" Nay not for him," she said, " alone I mourn,
Old gods dethroned may claim my tears and realms
Of beauty lost.   Change is the only fate.
Even gods are subject to his mighty sway.
Each moment works its will, and as men dream
That they are thus or thus, they cease to be
What they conceive themselves.   Who could have thought
That Greece would sink to what she is ? Proud Athens,
Home of ideal thought and noblest art —
Where now the poet, hero, sculptor, sage,
The men whose art prolongs the lives of god's,
Which keeps them in men's mouths when all their pomp
Of worship is no more : the words with wings ;
The graceful wisdom full of calm and smiles,
The pæans sounding thro' the laurels green
For ever, songs of joy which shook the dew
From pink and rose ?   Comes never more that life
To fill the world with worship, proudly make
All time its debtor ?   Where the Olympian fight
For no base sordid prize ?   Where are the men
Those billows gladly bore to fame and power,
Their triremes filled with valour fronting death,
While strains that still are living stirr'd the air ?
Gone like their shadows in the glassy deep !
Their very monuments oblivion's mockery.
That sea sounds doleful on desertless shores,
And glory's waters waste round voiceless isles.
No more, no, never, never more comes back
Upon the world such days, when men were men

All round, not narrow'd into specialisms,
When Æschylus fought and sang, when Pericles
Commanded armies, ruled the state, loved art,
And the bard's laurel kiss'd the victor's crown."
She waved her hand and on we went.   We dash'd
Against great banks of cloud and made them blaze,
And far ahead the skirts of flying Night
Were fring'd with silver lace, and round her neck
And swarthy bust a russet robe she cast
As though to shield her from day's prying eye.
O'er Salamis and Megaris we drove ;
A glance toward's Delphi's shrine and Dorian hills,
And Achaian vales renowned in ancient song,
And high Olympus once the throne of gods.
Ulysses' isle one moment claim'd our thoughts,
Then broke the sea upon the Apulian shore.
Canusium, Brundusium, Cannæ,
Arpi, Arpinum, these unnoticed pass'd.
We paus'd a moment o'er Imperial Rome,
Her tale   the Milky Way of mighty deeds,
Her streets a wilderness of monuments,
Her very dust made of the bones of saints ;
The Column, Forum, Coliseum, Arch,
Passed like the shadow of a bird.
                              " Ah there,"
I cried, " you have a theme."
                              " A theme indeed,"
She said, " on which I well might dwell, for none
Have loved to meet me more than those whose home
Was Rome.   Cæsar returning late from revel,
Power-musing, gazed upon the grey above

The Sabine Hills, noting with emulous eye
My conquering car across their summits flash ;
The capitol in purest outline stood
Against the steely background of the sky ;
The hum of life woke down the Sacred Way ;
The selfish clients throng'd the doors and halls
Of those proud nobles.   Mightiest and truest souls,
The tenderest spirits and noblest hearts,
Their highest inspirations find in me.
From Baiæ Horace oft Vesuvius' cone
Has watch'd grow red beneath my burning wheels,
And Virgil loved to see my eager steeds
Beat the dark ether into silver fire,
And hear the gentle breeze my rushing wheels
Send fragrant o'er the trembling forest trees.
Mine is the hour for meditation ; heart
And mind are freest ; care but half awake ;
Pale lust is drowsing ; blear-eyed drunkenness
Shrinks scared from me ; the soul she yearns to God ;
She feels her wings, like birds about to leave
The nest, and blesses Him who made all things
So fair !   The rose is ne'er so lovely-sweet
As when my rays gleam through the tremulous pearls
Within the shining ivory of its she'ls.
What time to watch the sea like that when o'er
Its steel-blue paths I drive, transforming sky
And wave, hiding in gleaming tissues gemmed,
Dawn's russet jerkin ?   Mine's the hour to think,
To pray, to hear great nature's heart beat.   He
Who'd know himself, know what and when to do,
Know what is best and fairest, what of power

Is in the step which walks with us, who'd draw
Into his life the forces of the gods,
Must greet me waking worlds from daily death.
A ressurrection comes with every dawn.
Yon glory-blazon'd city, black with crimes,

The mightiest stage on which mankind has play'd—
There the great battle was fought out afresh,
Christ crucified a thousand times—the rack,
The living torch, the wild beast's maw, the sword,
The myriad shout exultant of fierce joy
Within those Flavian walls, now ruin's home,
Then white with togas, sp'endid, beauty-crown'd,
Rank above rank, to watch the naked faith
Engage the world, nor dream'd that the poor slave
They doom'd had conquer'd death, and smote their **rule**
With truth's all deadly touch.   Gentle souls serene !
Their hymns, pure as the carols of the birds
Of dawn, I've heard mount o'er the Palatine,
While in the palace lust and madness gloom'd.
Long had our ancient lovely creeds decay'd—
The soulless relics of a by-gone day.
Their time was up.   I'd heard glad angels sing
In Bethlehem, had seen His after triumph,
Captivity led captive, Death in chains,
Just as the Jordan crimson'd in my ray,
But Olivet a glory wore which mine
Eclipsed.   I bow'd and reined my steeds until
Into the heaven of heavens He passed, the gates
Of God's supreme abode clang'd opening wide,
And shouts and songs of triumph shook the stars.
Him well I knew ; by Him I sprang to life ;

Like Pallas from the brain of Zeus full-arm'd
"Let there be light!" he said, and straight I was,
And driving 'thwart the limitless abyss,
Woke up old Chaos from eternal sleep,
And startled stars remote and farthest space
With the first footfalls of light's glancing feet.
Huge Darkness for a moment stood appal'd,
Then went, vague terror on his swarthy brow.
Alas? Christ's cult has been depraved.   Faithless,
Taking his cue from curiosity,
The priest, grown sceptical corrupts all creeds.
Weak men and weaker women fain would know
The future, tho' among its factor's will
Should hold no humble place.   They'd have the god
Some special favours to themselves afford,
Some better revelation of himself
Than starry spheres, than all earth's beauties teach
In form and tint, the sky-reflecting streams
Which feed the flower enamell'd odorous fields,
The lakes wherein the mountains glass their bulks
Majestic, looking greater in the wave,
Like lives of great ones passed away, whose word
Yet echoes in men's hearts, whose deeds still hold
The field against the blows of time.   Debased
Their pur-blind hearts conceive he'll come at call
Of spells in dim-lit holes, and that he loves
Oppressive smells, who makes wild trees and shrubs
To load the winds with perfume.   Fittest fane
For Him the boundless universe he made.
But men are children, various in their growth,
And so the soul be brought to touch with God's,

The end of all sincere religion's gained.
If man would reach the highest possible
He must, like Enoch, walk with God ; must build
His reservoir of power among the stars
If he would go as high ; who'd soar must feel
The strength divine within his life and hear
The unfaltering wings of fate beat time with his,
And, save such dread companionship, alone.
We minor gods our end subserv'd, but fail'd
To strike the master note of love, which chord
He struck evoking softest, sweetest strains,
With deeper spell than Orpheus' powerful lyre,
Which balm on hearts afflicted breathes and peace
On storm-tost souls, and more than martial airs
Can stir the hero's heart ; can nerve a chi'd
With gaze untroubled, frowning worlds to front ;
Its simple notes in purest accents heard,
And ancient crowns and creeds antique dissolve ;
The world for man new-born was made anew ;
Life throbb'd beneath the ribs of death ; new life
And full of joy in charnel hearts ; and o'er
Dominions of despair hope's shining star
Was seen, and sin was spurn'd.   Christ rais'd man high,
His own vain dreams have sunk him low."
She ceased and shook the silvery reins which flash'd
Like lightening bands above the Central Sea.
A southern breeze bore balm upon its wings
And shed Arabian perfume round our way.
" How fair this world," I cried.

               " Aye fair," she said,
" Fair the bright flowers whose eyes are fair for mine ;

Fair snowy falls and stream and fell and vale ;
The farmer faring nimbly to his fields,
His bucksome wife loud-chucking for her hens ;
The burly plowman turning up the earth ;
Small shapely fingers dressing loaded vines ;
The rooks at parley in the pine-tree tops ;
The orchestral bursts of joy from little throats
Of black-bird, thrush and robin, linnet, finch,
And lark — that rocket of heart-glowing song !
The sea - the free, the rushing waves at play ;
The steamship holding on 'gainst wind and tide ;
The sailor singing as he scours the deck ;
Fair is the mother praying with her babes ;
The boy, sly-creeping o'er his sleeping sire ;
The maiden in her lover's pure embrace,
Their trysting place the dewy fields of dawn ;
The ivied cottage whence the smoke up curls,
Its feet touched by the foam of sobbing seas ;
Fair is contrition's early prayer to heaven ;
Fair tender-handed nurses watching pain :
Fair holy nuns their orisons repeating ;
And fair the poet drinking in my force,
Framing great songs whose waves melodious bear
High thoughts like ships rich laden.   Fair all these,
But I could show you where ghast murder glares,
Terror with all her furies standing near ;
Where at this hour which seems so fair to you,
Bewilder'd girls drown their helpless babes ;
Where women beautiful as Dian's smile
In silver seas, drowse guilty in gilt splendour,
Or sleep the outworn thralls of lust ; men dower'd

With Fortune's favours, yes and those with gifts
Of mind, in drunken langour snoring life
Away ; gaunt hunger crimp'd in garrets vile ;
The moon-light ruffian coming from his work
Of savage war on civil life ; and here
A mountain side, a peasant's hut, his home
Where he and his were born, but whence vile greed
Ejects him now unjustly, for it made
His load too heavy.   He in anger scowls ;
The aged palsied mother weeps ; the wife
With apron wipes her tears away ; then scolds
The instruments of law, to them the dogs
Of pitiless oppression ; sons tall, strong,
With murderous eye survey the bailiff hard ;
The children cry, the neighbours helpless crowd
Against the cordon thrown around by power.

    Aye fair the world ! but did I make you see
The ceaseless, measureless flow of heart-wrung tears,
And hear the chorus vast of woeful sighs !
Fair were this world, were but mens' actions fair.
But now—"

    Quick moved her hand, a gesture proud
Of scorn.   The lightning gleam'd within her eyes
Deep blue ; crimson her cheek, her nostrils spread ;
But pity driving anger out she cried :
" Poor man ! not wholly hateful even at worst,
At best, he's greater than the gods themselves.
The poet and priest have praised us long in song
More laden with coarse flattery than altars
With fat of lamb and ram and bullock, for they deem'd
We loved the odour which your dainty dame

Will faint to find invade her boudoir.   Now
A god will say a word in praise of man —
We are immortal.   Man's frail life a whiff
From swamp or river puffs out ; all the odds
Against achievement ; his rewards they grow
Upon the precipice's ledge ; he toils,
Fails, fights again for doubtful prizes, plucks
His flowers with wide-mouth'd ruin gaping far
Below ; he lives and sweats for other men,
Whose tardy praises will not reach his ears.
He thinks, he acts, he laughs, he weeps, he loves,
And always in death's shadow ; whatever house
He builds, his destined lodging is the tomb.
The bride he wreaks his heart on, death will claim,
And make a grinning horror of the face
Which thrilled his soul.   The dome where genius dwells
And whence it sends its thoughts, like arms, to clasp
The universe, becomes a hideous piece
Of crumbling bone.   Yet on the isthmus small
Of life, the past and future, like great seas
On either hand whose deeps oblivious
Devouring all, make mockery of fame,
What works, what plans immense the insect rears !
We see fruition ; we the end enjoy ;
Ten thousand heroes walk the earth and sow
And know they cannot reap, but those they love
Will—mother, wife or child ; ten thousand who
Would gladly die for men they never knew.
Such lives, such deeds, the noblest praise for him
Whose fingers form'd wondrous man.

All Europe lay beneath us now ; a map
Whereon since Cæsar's time change scribbles, like
A wayward child perverse ; red battle fields
As thick as tomb-stones in the parish ground,
And armies that in thunder yet will break
On bloodier fields.

          More silvery grey the clouds
Above and round the city of the Seine.
Clear did it show in regular beauty fair.
Clear showed its long straight streets with boskage lined ;
Its boulevards, and palaces and towers
And domes, and thro' the wilderness of art,
Beneath its many ponts, between its wealth
Of trees umbrageous, the river moved ;
The cab its light—a pin head, plied for hire ;
From Neuilly and well-cultur'd Courbevoie
The market cart came 'neath the Arc de Triomphe,
And, looking like a beetle, hurried down
The Champs Elysées, which contrasted now,
In the pure quiet of the early dawn,
With the coarse splendours of its nightly wont.
Empty those gardens where vain pleasure haunts,
Where queens of lust to-day in diamonds shine,
Who on no distant morrows die in rags.
The Boulevardian roar is hushed ; the blaze
Of Cafés veiled ; of thrice ten thousand shops
The glory's out ; but all that soul can stir
Remains : The dome which rises o'er his tomb
Who broke on Europe bearing death and fire,
And carrying terror to the hearts of kings,
Whole nations mesmerizing, whose column stands

And Arch Triumphant, reverenced by those
Who would all else destroy.   That gilded dome
Shines like another sun, and there lies he
Silent, but still a wonder and a power.
Yet more inspiring are the monuments
Which speak of death to tyrants and of hope
For men, of aspirations after good,
The love of liberty, the love of man,
The love of art, of song.   Yes! Paris stands
By suffering purified, with more true force
To raise men's thoughts than when false glitter call'd
From every side proud dissolute wealth,
To dazzle thro' the streets of slaves.

                                           She read
My thoughts, and, answering them, the goddess spake :
" Amazing genius in the Kelt abides.
How sweet his warm, quick, gentle courtesy !
How brave in arms !   Excelling in all arts !
How loyal to the leader of his heart !
His very vanity a power.   The price
He pays for his great gifts is great : balance,
The steady aim and duty made supreme.
France might be well content to-day.   She lost
But what she took by force.   But thunders crouch
In every heart.   Ere long they'll Rhine-ward spring.
And, though the fight will not be such as when
A court of cowards and cocottes held sway,
'Twill end disastrously for France.   Her foe
Has all the great conditions of success.
The people *will* be made ambition's pawns,
Ten thousand bleed to make one leader great,

Perhaps to make a tyrant ; such is man ;
Of all his follies war's red glory worst.
If wisdom ruled, the peoples of the world
Might be as one."
                The isles of freedom lay
Like jewels on the ocean's breast.   The roar
Of London now was still.   Its million flues
Had not yet thrown a canopy opaque
Between it and the sky.   A thousand spires
Rose clear into the air.   Their crosses shone.
Huge chimneys hideous forms reared above
The sea of roofs, and, like a penitent,
The Tower, full of remorseful memories, showed.
The river seemed to slumber on its way ;
Its shores of new embankment, buildings old,
St. Paul's great dome, St. Stephen's ornate tower,
Were mirrored in its calm but murky tide.
Huge barges lay, like monsters of the deep
Asleep.   Ten thousand masts were tipp'd with gold.
'Twas fancy, or I heard the ghost-like tread
Of stray policemen in deserted streets.
A speck, the waggon laden with fresh fruits
And roots and flowers, towards Covent garden moved.
A blot of wretchedness crept down the strand,
Another night of sin and gin and pain
Gone by.   Slow limpt she to her squalid home,
If home was hers in that hard populous hive.

  " There," said my guide, " the largest city time
E'er saw, the seat of peerless empire, built
By valorous deeds and counsels sage, now caught
In the fierce draw of wild democracy,

Whose rapids menace death.   Founder she will
Amongst those howling rocks unless the wise
And patriot rule the hour.   The House of Lords—
A scuttled, mastless hulk in stormy seas.
The boasted constitution's gone, and England,
Unless she builds anew, 'gainst perils new
Will split up in the roaring surge.   The man
Of state to-day who wins success is he
Who rattles loudest for the monstrous child,
With headlong passions and imperial power.
Poor tricks are played.   Any bait to which
The fish will rise.   Great men of long renown
Palter with truth, and seek, like circus clowns,
To ride two horses ; daub themselves and lose
Identity.   What they are, what next
They'll do, no man can say.   They'll summersault,
Or jump through all their principles.   They'll fall,
They'll tumble, then up smiling come, and bow
For cheers, that Burke had rather die than hear.
A few, indeed, the danger see.   The rest
Sing songs of progress, or in dalliance live,
Deaf to the ruin-thundering billows near.
The greatest and the noblest nation, too,
That's risen yet should not so fall."   She ceased.

   "Is that small isle," I asked, "whose earth-fenced fields
Gleam emerald from below, the land of Flood
And Grattan ?"

          Answering she sighed, or seem'd
To sigh :   "Yes ; that's Ierne there."

                "O stained,"
I cried, "with centuries of tears and crimes

Recriminating crimes, what hope for her ?   .
Must she forever lie a floating sorrow
On heaven upbraiding seas ?   Will never fall
From skies of mercy healing dews for her !
No power e'er break the spell of anarchy ?
And fill the land with happy homes and men
Made truly free from wrong by rectitude,
And balanc'd judgment pointing to what's fit ?"
"That land," she said, "will also have its day.
Fail'd, fail'd, ignominiously they've failed
To whom the glorious privilege of rule
Was given.   Lost in low frivolity,
On them were lost high opportunities.
They spent, drank, sank and soddened into swine,
Or lived, bloodhounds and beagles, chasing whom
They should protect.   No sense at all of duty.
Their highest art to run a fox to death,
Harrying a hare their noblest day's delight ;
The peasant girl a quarry for their lusts ;
License their law, and blind to skyey portents,
They ground who'll now grind them ; their wisdom's thrift
To blight the land of which they were the lords.
The hour of retribution comes, and time's
Old ledger evens up accounts.   To-day
In freedom's happy land th' evictor's child
Bows to the evicted's, and low-cringing sues
For palty place--so terrible is Fate !
The danger's now men may mistake the cry
Of blinding Vengeance for the voice of Justice.
If headlong hate's hot counsels shall prevail,
And truth and honesty be nosed aside,

As swine would pearls, then comes the hour of fate
For those who stand elate on victory's steps,
Nor weigh the duties favouring gods impose.
Wolf-like attacks on one defenceless man,
The cruel boycott piled on travails pangs,
The sinless heifer hock'd by senseless hands,
The yet green harvest mow'd with envy's scythe,
The worst of tyrannies in worst of forms,
A reign of terror through the country side,
The honest farmer who will dare be just,
Is either slain by brother peasants' hands
Or earless drives his tailless kine to town —
Such deeds, tho' fruits of misused power — for not
The money taken from the land, the trim
Spruce agent gutting huts, the agony
Of bursting hearts that dared not speak, embrace
The worst ; the degradation of the man
O'er-shadows all : yet none the less such deeds
The name of freedom soil and balk the aim
Of those who'd bring in better happier days.
E'en God's aims fail because of man's misdeeds.
This only certain, Goodness, Truth, the Right
Prevail at last.   But man his own best star
Can be his own worst bale.   Once give him power
Forgot are all the lessons of all times,
He yokes himself to passion, heaven provokes
To send on him the plague which crush'd his foes.
Yet hope's star rises o'er that troubled land.
A healthy breeze comes from her stormy sky,
Will blow down bigotry's corrupting shrines,
Her fatuous feuds the nightmare of vain dreams

Of day's delusive and of ways defiled
By deeds ill-suited to the present hour.
She'll play a part her world-scatter'd sons
Can watch, nor blush : Empire's right hand ; her soil
No longer drain'd to deck the Paris jade ;
Security where dark assassins lurk'd ;
Fields laden with earth's bounty where high walls
Uprear'd by pride, wide-barrenness enclosed ;
Contentment on the yeoman's ruddy face,
Within his heart the glow of charity
For all the brother peoples of the earth,
And decent self-respect where pig and ass
Were hous'd on equal terms with man."

                    She ceased ;
The horses forward sprang ; the Atlantic broad
Was well in view.   The chariot flying o'er
The watery plain, bright roads of purple wide
Were dashed this way and that

                    O ! the pulsing sense
Of life exstatic ! O the wide, wide sea !
The sea-gulls wheel and poise and dip for prey,
The porpoise bounding through the billows, whales
Shooting to heaven great towers of glittering spray,
Their brown backs heaving huge above the wave,
Like boats upturn'd.   What joy to sail for ever
High o'er the dark blue sea !"   And Eos spake :

    " I've told you of man's greatness," said the goddess
" Amaze and admiration fill your soul
At this wide sweep of measureless sea
Now all but calm.   Some day you may again

Stray o'er these waters by my side, when clouds
Will wrap my car, clouds crashing thunder ;   hail
And lightening flaring round our heads ; the bolt
Of Jove, wild hissing in the mad abyss,
And then unharm'd for I will throw my shield
Invisible twixt death and you, you will admire,
For you have lov'd the storm whose choral music,
Long-pealing thro' aerial aisles, has been
To you from infancy a joy.   I've seen
Upon the sea, what all surpassed itself
In storm or calm : men save lives and die,
Nor blench with all its fury hurtling round
Their heads serene ; Columbus crossing ways
Untrodden, guided by bold thought and faith,
And mark'd him quell his mutinous men and move
Heroic in his slender craft, unawed
By man or elements, and reach his gaol
Despite of faltering fickle hearts ; despite
The warring dread white-banner'd billows vast,
The hurtling, roaring, spar-shaking, sibilant seas,
As in battalions up they rose to bar
The invader.   Toils, privations, envy cares,
Ingratitude, neglect, the scorn of fools,
Successful treachery, contempt and want,
All this was his for throwing wide the gates
Not only of new lands with wealth untold,
But of an era new for down-crush'd man.
For liberty required a virgin soil.
What has Columbus done for Europe's slaves !
Not only for the homeless happy homes ;
With the small leaven of great pioneers,

It made and makes from Europe's ooze and scum,
The foremost nation in fair freedom's ranks.
It's citizens—they walk the earth like kings.
Proud self-reliant, they have stript the crest
From idleness and swept from toil the ban,
And for the brave and strong thrown all doors wide.
There is the field of victory over kings
And tyrants, aye, and o'er the passions wild
Of the impulsive throng. The courtly mob
May sneer, but no where else the crowding mass
Of men have been erect and free, each man
A sovereign, knowing this, respecting all,
However poor, who bravely work their way,
Not capable of bending pliant knees,
Or doffing cap to any child of earth."

We noted soon great ice-bergs floating like
Abandoned isles and curving round the shores
Of Nova Scotia, Anticosti, New
Brunswick, Prince Edward and Quebec, the waves
Of the St. Lawrence Gulf with refluent sweep;
The fishing fleets like fairy tents encamped
Upon the plains, and schools of mackarel
Moved shoreward shining in a thousand hues,
While o'er them boiled the sea or seemed to boil.

We reached, admired and pass'd that city hoar
Which wears an old face in a world all new,
From whose high plain and storied citadel,
Wolfe's glory streams for ever, and we mark'd
How the broad river roll'd along, wide-hemmed
With wooded shores, the land and water all

One mighty maze of ruby sun-'it mist,
Far-burning wood and sheets of silver fire.
A shade of thought passed like a cloudlet o'er
Her face, and like a summer cloudlet went.
" Lo ! there," she said, "a piece of French antique
'Gainst which the waves of time its blasts and storms
Would seem to break in vain. They cling down there
To forms and glories and traditions old
Of other lands and of long-vanished years,
And while they live beneath one rule, they own
The civilization of another, not
In harmony therewith ; nor can they cease
To look beyond the sea until that day,
Far off, which impulse new will give and bind
The heart's affections round the land they till,
Their mother then, no nursing substitute
For one long leagues away. They have the force,
They have the genius of a mighty race ;
Poets and thinkers, statesmen eloquent ;
Their peasants gentle, virtuous folk ; but lost
Are many winning graces of the Gaul
At home. Old wine is pent in bottles new ;
You see the same faults farther west in those
Blind egotists, who damn in others what
They do themselves the merest slaves of cant,
Of what has been—incapable of deeds
Strong-limbed and bold, such as are born of thought
And will. But there shall come a race in which
This Gallic stream will play a noble part,
A race, which gathering strength from diverse founts,
Will— a majestic river—onward flow,

Full volumn'd, vast, its guide its proper bent,
And take its character and hues from all
That makes the present great – rolling along
A crowded avenue of wealth and power.

She shook the reins which gleam'd like lightning bands,
The horses toss'd their meteor heads, the clouds
Flew round their feet in darting flames, the mist
Rose up illuminated round our wake,
Which blazed a diamond track for many a league.
Upon my brow the wind was cold ; I heard
The rush of wheels so quick each look'd a fire
Of dazzling brightness ; held by power divine
I held my place.

    But now she drew the reins
Tight, and the horses stopped.   I heard the singing
Of tributary streams, and looking down
Saw where the river – the Ottawa –cut out
Of the eldest ribs of earth a theatre vast.
Like threads of silver run from silver coin
To coin, it wound between the hills, and spread
At intervals in wide and beauteous lakes.

Right in the midst a hill fit throne for rule,
And crowning this were stately structures, towers
And domes and gothic arches quaint, with rich
Device of ornament.   A shade of grave
Reflection passed across her face but did
Not mar the outlines of immortal youth,
Nor dim its hues.   Her eyes looked far away
As though all future time was glass'd within

Their depths : so look'd the Cumæan Sibyl's,
Her first convulsion o'er, when she foretold
Æneas all the years held in their womb
For his descendants.

        "These," she said, " were built
By one of large conceptions, forecast sage,
Imperial dreams, in whom Ulyssean wiles
Were wedded with a grasp for state affairs
Which mates him with those mighty minds whose care
And patient wisdom nations found : great souls,
Whose monuments are continents, from whom
Whole races drink their inspiration.
He had to work with crude materials gross,
His task to wield in one wide-scatter'd states.
Abroad, at home, fat ignorance beset
His path : the smug sagacity of men
Purblind, —the chosen voice of those ill fit
To choose who shall declare what law must be -
The roar of calumny, faction's furious feuds,
The want of heart, of faith, proper to times
When Mammon-worship is the shameless cult
Of most,—with these and more he had to fight,
But he nor blench'd nor faltered one small hour,
But like a law bore on, borne up by hopes
Such as are parents of immortal things."

She ceased.   The sense's memory, tremulous with
Her tones, like some rare music often heard
Before, with happy pain my heart made faint,
And in my eyes the waves well'd up from founts
Of joy and grief ; the chords of mourning thrill'd

As for some loss divine, while all the springs
Of rapture moved; meanwhile thro' tears I mark'd
The rosy bulge of delicate clouds which slept
On either side.   She said:

       "Lo beautiful lives
Dissolved in mist and rocked asleep by airs
Impalpable as they."

      "But up there came
The phantom roar of waters.   Bending o'er
The car which now was near the earth, I saw
Where over rocks wild torrents gnashed and foam'd,
And I was noting how the mass of white
And furious billows, catching rays of dawn,
Began to show like a great rose in vase
Of silver, fringed with jasmin flowers, when she
Went on:

      "Yes, there's the seat of empire young,
A people destin'd to be great and free,
Tho' oft blind ignorance and greed these halls
Invade, and in fair Freedom's very fane
Swine guttle.   Ah ! these eyes have seen what man
Can do.   Full many a morning have I watch'd
The envious croud in Athens spit out hate
Of noble Pericles, the balanc'd man,
Wise with all wisdom, beautiful with love
Of every art, who made Athena's home
Worthy of her—that light for evermore
To man; for sink he ne'er so low, the hog
In him may overgrow the soul, and lust
And drunkenness drive far the graceful forms
Which wait on the pure life, still must he rise

Again, redeemed, drawn by the power of Athens —
Her beauty fairer than the lover dreams
Of her he loves —the greatness of the mind,
Calm, self contained; the music struck by souls
For goodness passionate from nature's strings,
The scorn of death, the love of noble deeds—
All this will rest on mankind like a spell,
And spite of filth and crime, disease and death,
Cause them to move towards excellence   Ah ! true,
The course is slow.   The freshening morning comes
Upon the heels of night and gives each day
A new birth to the world; the years steal by
And leave behind their legacies of fact;
The generations rise and fall like waves,
But ere they die the store of knowledge swell;
The centuries bearing names and deeds of note,
And petty pangs and lyric joys and loves
Too weighty for frail lives —the centuries flee;
A thousand years are gone like yesterday;
Old empires sink into decreptitude;
New kingdoms rise; even races pass away;
New types appear; new forms of civic life —
But man is still the same blind fool, the same
Base groveller, still will he hug his chains,
And still pursue what leads to chains and death.
Down the ruining precipices of time
Tyrant and tyrannies are hurled, and man
A moment rises free and stands erect;
The future opens like a dawn of spring;
It seems as if afar in depths of space
The stars were harping choral symphonies,

In sympathy with worlds born again,
And a new era stood upon the verge
Of fact.　Alas!　Vile use has bred the slave's
Habit:　The horse has flung his rider off,
But runs bewilder'd till another holds
The reins, and makes him feel the master's touch;
The late wash'd sow grows sad with cleanliness,
But as the pig imagination glows
With dreams of wallowing near, she grunts with joy.
Ruled by Pisistratus men could not be
Worse slaves than they are there in that young land,
In this new world.　They have academies;
And from a thousand tabernacles gleams
The cross, the symbol sweet of truths more deep
Than Greek philosophy, or modern lore.
They have the garner'd wealth of ages old
And new, but cannot think—the serfs of bold
And blatant calumny, whose breath of life
Is rank vituperation of the best
And wisest men.　That form of civic life
Which liberty and government by the sage
Secures, nowhere in that round world is seen.
Democracy puts apes in power, and howls
Hosannas praising not humility
Divine an ass bestriding, but the ass
Himself, out-braying hideous egotisms,
Richly comparison'd and capering o'er
The prostrate crowd, while those who live, the salt
Of human things, who keep society
From mortifying, hated are push'd
Aside; low cunning more and more is crown'd.

Without some practice, who can plough a field?
Without instruction, who can make a watch?
Without much study, who can master art?
But men will act as if the veriest boor
Were fit for government, while government
Of all things man can do is hardest, most
Beset with problems such as only minds
Of finest fibre, trained and confident
From knowledge and the sense of power can cope
With   Give to poor small brains the task to drive
This chariot, Phaethon's fate awaits him, worse
Than Phaethon's fate, perhaps, the people whom
He tries to rule.   But still things onward move;
And though the curve that's near will seem depraved,
And is, in times's large circles progress lives;
And 'tis permitted generous hope to keep,
That in a far off day the dull will honour
Worth with other meed than hate.   The heart
Of mediocrity will sweetened be
By sweet benevolences born of time
And sad experience.   Benefactors wise
Of men will then not have to wait till death
For their reward; but many a lapsing year
Must pass, before the harp from which the Fates
Will strike this music has been made, and oh!
How many thousand times my burning wheels
Will lighten o'er this earth before I can
Announce that happy morn.   Right under here
The savage ruled, and on that very hill
His councils held, councils which in the mind
Of Jove rank near as high as those which now

A race self-styled superior hold, alone
In cunning great.   They do not feed on dogs
Or human flesh, but moral cannibals
They are.   They kill with venomous lies and then
Like ghouls they batten on the corpse, and scenes
Humiliating as an Indian dance
Around a white dog swimming in its broth,
Have been enacted in that chamber where
A Cicero should find himself at home,
And Burke's deep wisdom be a common thing.
Who worships truth? who honours liberty?
A few.   Too few.   The mass are lost in love
Of gain, in low desires, conceptions all
Unworthy of the task they should essay.
Talk statesmanship to them, you cast your pearls
Away ; but rave and slaver out abuse
And they will crunch the hardest epithets,
With joy the garbage bolt, and gulp the swill
Of reeking rhetoric."

    Her cheek here seem'd
To burn as with a touch of angry red.
The reins she shook which flashed like lightening bands
Along the horses' backs.   Like fire when winds
Are strong, whole streets ablaze, roofs crashing in,
The sky red-hot, the roar as of mad seas
At war, the firemen's toil in vain —like fire
They forward sprang, and, in a twinkling, towers
And blocks of masonry majestical
Looked like a doubtful edifice of dreams,
Dim, air-built castles of forgotten years ;
The cataract a second glanc'd —a gleam

Of white 'gainst rainbow dust ; the lakes swept by,
Reflecting now the forms of fiery steeds,
And now a rosy shadow, and again
The gem-like radiance of our burnish'd trail.
She reined her horses, turn'd her head and said :
" How beautiful must that fair city be
When o'er Laurentian hills Apollo sinks !"

" O Eos, splendid in thy gleam !" I said,
" 'Tis far more beautiful at sunset hours,
And at that time upon the river oft
A song is heard, which should your gentle ear
Not scorn a mortal's voice, I'll sing.   I sang,
And as I sang the air was play'd by hands
Unseen on some mysterious harp divine .—

" Fair is the sight, when sinking to his rest,
The sun leans gently on the mountain's breast,
Empurpled clouds his radiant limbs bedeck,
And golden curls hang round his glossy neck.
The enamour'd river flushes in his gaze,
And every westward window is ablaze ;
And every tower and turret gleams awhile
In the warm radiance of his parting smile ;
And every drop that Chaudière flings on high,
One moment wears a gold or Tyrian dye ;
And every soul by nature finely wrought,
Is touch'd till feeling becomes one with thought,
And thought is rapture, like some moon-drawn sea,
The brimming spring-tide of eternity
Within the breast, on which the soul sets sail,

And leaves this world with its allurements stale ;
And when at last the sun is lost to sight,
And the pale moon looks wistful for the night,
Along those tracts of heaven where he has passed,
Great gorgeous draperies of clouds are massed ;
Or war seems there, with all its carnage dire,
Buildings in flames and battlements on fire.
You think you hear the sonorous trumpet's swells,
The roar of cannon and the whizz of shells ;
Or tints so tender linger in the sky,
The heart o'er-flows and wets the raptur'd eye,
And blesses him who taught the soul to know
Such heavenly beauty in this world below ;
For in the soul is all the beauty there
And without love 'tis so much empty air.
The purple fades ; more bright the moon beams shine ;
Beneath the deep'ning blue a saffron line
Alone recalls the pageantry and power,
The boisterous splendors of that sunset hour ;
The saffron's lost in ultra-deep marine,
And starry Night is mistress of the scene !"

" Ah that's a sight," she said, " I fain would see,
But even the gods must limit their desires."

    O'er all Ontario's wealth of field and town
The music followed, and still breath'd around
When Lake Superior spread below, it's isles
Of bosky beauty fragrant, mirror'd clear ;
At last the prairie wide, with tint of flower
As delicate as her own cheek.

                                    We paused,
The broad brown prairie hollowed-out beneath.
" Monotonous," she cried, " yet like the sea."
I said : " Its beauty must be seen from earth,
Its dazzling, glowing skies all clear of cloud
And fervent with the sun-god's strongest beams,
Or strewn with soft white pillows tier on tier ;
Like swans at rest upon a sea of blue,
They rise from rim to top o' the sky's great womb,
Fruitful of beauty, gendering all the wealth
Of yellow grain and roots, and all green things,
The flowers that shine as if sun-rays took root,
And shredded stars in balmy dewy nights
Were broadcast sown to be the stars of earth :
Blue bells, the sun-flower small and great, the rose,
The crocus and anemome, the wild
Convolvulus, and thousands more I love,
And daily scent and see but cannot name ;
Or when the Storm broods and his wide wings g'ower
O'er all the vast expanse of level land,
Which cowers, grows darker, flatter under the black
Terror of dread thunder-quivering pinions,
Death-stricken by the wild far-flashing fire,
Arm'd with swift death and splendours from his eye,
And by the voice of him which breaks like seas
That rise to make a universal wreck,
And bellow ruin, deafening remotest stars,
Then fails afar on the shrinking, shuddering air,
Dying in murmurs of loud discontent
And anger, like a world muttering pain,
Amid the blazing agonies of collapse,

And making kindred planets blink with fear;
Or in the clear bright days of Autumn's glow,
The gracious bracing time, spirit and balm
In every breath and breeze, when even the blast
Has some soft touch of sweetness, and every pulse
Glows with a thrill of rapture, and to live
Is joy ; its superb sunset pageantries,
When large and yellow suns go down aflame
'Mid tapestries immense of purple clouds,
And continents of vapour, their vast hearts
On fire; the russet purple and silver rise
Of suns which grow all gold within an hour,
Wide-gleaming, splendid, indescribable,
In spring time, or in harvest when the seas
Of golden grain shine like the golden fleece,
Or in mid winter, all the sky clear, glad,
The purple-hollowed crust of wide white plain,
O'er which and thwart the trail of dazzling light,
The powder'd snow, in forms fantastic, skips
To music of the northern blast, and skims
Away and never turns in that wild waltz,
Not for a thousand miles; the sluggard then,
With feet on stove and pipe in mouth, his blood
Bakes, while the man whose blood is pure and rich,
Flesh and muscle and nerve and heart in tune
With the clear spirit that bears up his life,
Revels in stimulating airs, and drinks
The cold pure ether, stirring high the heart
Like wine. Clad in thick furs, he drives or walks,
And, feeling exaltation, gathers power.
In early winter comes a day all sun,

While every shrub is thick with silver frost.
The air, like choicest champagne, thrills your veins.
No place so fit to watch the wheeling stars,
And see the northern lights illume the dark.
The soft night's solemn stillness fills with awe
The fragrant air, the soul with other worlds;
And tho' no trees can tempt the pensive moon
To tarry o'er their tops, her course she holds
In the wide silence of a prairie night
'Mid stars that seem to peer more close to earth,
And all as sweetly lures to contemplation,
And fills with passions calm, yet fiery strong,
A feeling weird unutterably deep,
As when on Latmos down she came to kiss
Endymion's lips, her lovely fingers white
Within his locks of lavish gold, the while his breath
Glow'd fast and warm upon her pale-flushed cheek,
And set her lips aflame ; or when she charm'd
Orion ere on Merope he gazed,
Or thou exultantly to Delos bore
His mighty beauty for secure retreat.
In vain!   Her jealous arrows found him there.

    "Speak not of him," she said, "I saw him lie
The mourning billows breaking at his feet,
A hundred shafts swift rooted in his breast ; his face
Pale, tortured ; while cold Dian paler moved,
With tranquil triumph smiling, as my team
Made the raw ether burn like my brow."

She sigh'd, a sigh of recollected pain,
And said: " I'll play the gadding gossip for
Your sake to-day.   See where the iron horse
Pants, puffs out smoke and snorts and cries and bears
Long trains thro' what was wilderness a year
Ago; flinging his smoke aloft he makes
A passing cloud.   Upon these plains immense
Where here and there the signs of man at work
Are seen, it is but yesterday the red
Man, the poor savage chased the buffalo.
I've seen him in his prime and his decay;
But save the wild ox and his pursuers
This land has been a solitude since it
Was heaved up from the sea.   For centuries ?—
Oh! yes, for thousands, those bright lakes have shone
Unmark'd; the wild ducks lived upon their breasts
Nor feared the fowler's shot ; the roses bloomed ;
The gopher dug his hole and stood erect,
And ran and lived his lonely graceful life,
And played among the grasses and the flowers;
The ground-lark sang; the prairie hen and plover
Their broods unharmed reared; the antelope
At times a prize to the Indian's arrow fell;
The wolf at all hours prowled in search of prey ;
But not a trace of man, save when the chase
Brought savage hunters from the river's marge,
The beautiful wooded vales of the Qu'Appelle,
Saskatchewan, and streams subsidiary.
The Indian's doom should touch your heart.   I've seen
Tpyes disappear before.   But kindness
On dying races, as on dying men

Should wait, and Canada may well be proud,
And England, too, of that just spirit which
Has ruled her councils; these are things the gods
Do not forget."

         " I'd fear," I said, " this seat
To hold in winter when wide snow shrouds all
The vasty plain.   But once more, that's the time
To watch from earth your car speed on.   The snow
In wind-made waves lies like a frozen sea,
And in their myriad hollows shadows cast,
Their clear-cut million-faceted backs agleam,
Light-darting, radiant in thy rosy smile;
The heaven a dappl'd glory.   Soon the rim
Of burning gold with radiating spears
Peeps up, then slowly sails in yellow seas
Of light, the full orb'd splendour whence
There runs across the white empurpled sea
Like fire, to the entranced gazer's feet,
A lane of silver fire, and all the plain
Compact of tiniest crystals flames with gems;
Diamonds and chrysolites bespangling blaze;
The frosty heavens high-up, gold fretted, blue,
Save where some pearly clouds may westward rest,
Which half an hour before were crimson round
Your wheels.   The air the pulses stirs like fire
And life's a joy !"

         She smiled and said : — " Yes, cold
No doubt for mortal brow, the swift sharp air
Which up here whistles on my wintery way.
I love myself to gaze upon those plains
When bright auroraborealian tints

Go flashing flame-wise o'er their snowy waves,
More gorgeous in their bright commingling hues
Than cunningest mystery of colours quaint
In old cathedral windows, shedding gloried light
Thro' pillar'd silent aisles.   But lo! the sun
Comes on apace.   We must not further pause."

   The reins she shook, which flash'd like lightning bands,
And forward rushed those coursers wild, and wheels
Of fire, and soon the snowy peaks of hills
So high, our horses airy feet might well
Have touch'd the topmost, were empurpled.   Cones
Which rose at frequent intervals, grew pink
And red, white clefts and chasms fathom-deep
Gloomed dark and dreadful.   The eagle was awake
And wheel'd with sail-broad pinions strong, in search
Of quarry; back and wings to us seem'd like
Gilt bronze of antique armour worn by knights
Of old, on which flames out the light of fire
In some baronial hall hung round with casques,
And breast-plates, shields, and shirts of mail and spears
Transverse; the founder of the house he glowers
Above the hearth huge as cathedral door.
The eagle's shadow on the white peak's side
Was as the shade of some long-pointed cloud
When winds are veering.

                    Now the Fraser gleam'd
Below, its benches white with apple trees
In bloom.   'Neath one an Indian stood, in hand
A tom-tom rude, on which he beat, the while

He sang in sad tones looking towards the sea.
The children of his tribe impassive sat
And smoked their deep-bowl'd long-stemmed pipes.

With spread wings for ever
  Time's eagle careers,
His quarry old nations,
  His prey the young years;
Into monuments brazen
  He strikes his fierce claw,
And races are only
  A sop for his maw.

The red sun is rising
  Behind the dark pines,
And the mountains are marked out
  In saffron lines,
The pale moon still lingers,
  But past is her hour
Over mountain and river
  Her silver to shower.

As yon moon disappeareth,
  We pass and are past;
The pale face o'er all things
  Is potent at last.
He bores thro' the mountains,
  He bridges the ford,
He bridles steam horses
  Where Bruin was lord,

He summons the river
　Her wealth to unfold,
From flint and from granite
　He crushes the gold.

Those valleys of silence
　Will soon be alive
With huxters who chaffer,
　Prospectors who strive,
And the house of the pale face
　Will peer from the crest
Of the cliff, where the eagle
　To-day builds his nest.

The Red Skin he marred not
　White fall on wild rill,
But to-morrow those waters
　Will turn a mill;
And the streamlet which flashes
　Like a young squaw's dark eye,
Will be black with foul refuse,
　Or may be run dry.

From the sea where the Father
　Of waters is lost,
To the sea where all Summer
　The ice-berg is tost,
The white hordes will swarm
　And the white man will sway,
And the smoke of his engine
　Make swarthy the day.

Round the mound of a brother
  In sadness we pace,
How much sadder to stand
  At the grave of a race !
But the good Spirit knows
  What for all is the best,
And which should be chosen
  The strife or the rest.

As for me, I'm time-weary,
  I await my release,
Give to others the struggle,
  Grant me but the peace,
And what peace like the peace
  Which Death offers the brave?
What rest like the rest
  Which we find in the grave?

For the doom of the hunter
  There is no reprieve;
And for me, 'mid strange customs,
  'Tis bitter to live.
Our part has been played
  Let the white man play his;
Then he too disappears,
  And goes down the abyss.
Yes ! Time's eagle will prey
  On the Pale Face at last,
And his doom like our own
  Is to pass and be past.

He closed exultantly, in contrast strange
To mien and tone with which he had begun.
The grandeur, gloom, and dread sublimity
Of this great river was soon left behind.
We passed o'er lucid streams whose sands are gold:
Inlets and gulfs whose beauty man can ne'er
Destroy; forests of mighty trees whose age
You count by tens of centuries, and now
Reflecting many a shape—outlines too fair
For gross embodiment in flesh—young forms
Of tender beauty, robed in hues of heaven,
Attendant on that glory-scattering car,
The rippleless ocean lay beneath us, bright;
No wrinkle on its vast and placid brow;
No cloud in view, and as we flew along
Deep voices from around the car poured forth
Sweet strains which o'er the ocean rolled and died
In frozen whispers 'mid the polar seas.

"This is the sea," she said, "on which a bard
Might feel the inspiration of your empire,
And write an epic worthy of the race
Or races which have built it grandly up;
For Kelt and Saxon, each has done his share;
By Kelt and Saxon, must it be maintained.
The Irish on a hundred battle fields,
In counsel by the spoken word, by toil,
Have play'd a great part in this work.
They should have scope to bless their own green isle;
But shipwreck will attend their aims, unless
They merge them in a noble loyalty

To the gre t empire which is theirs no less
Than others? Poor wailing round old graves
And cries for vengeance, show how deep all wrongs
Will strike, and hers were of the greatest: long
Continued, cruel, cold, calamitous
Injustice, poison'd with contempt and scorn
Engend'ring hate. But heroes do not waste
Themselves upon the past -- on dead things gone;
The present and the future, there's their field.
Those isles are link'd by Fate; the people lords,
'Tis theirs to learn the cause of all is one,
Or from their wrangles, flames will shoot and wrap
The edifice, and in the general blaze
Both crash in ruin. War to the idler, war
To all injustice, war to faction, war
To gilt corruption, war to agitation,
Its work once done, and love like fruitful heaven
Spanning these lands, and then it will be seen
How much of greater greatness was within
The grasp of Britain than her past can show.
Your young Dominion, by imperial works
Worthy an ancient state, built up by one
As yet in gristle, nobly aids the task,
And gives large promise of the mightier day."

The ocean was now left behind -- a breadth
Of light. A score of dusky nations old
We pass, then plunge beneath the engulphing waves.
A rush of waters green and white-- again
I clos:d my eyes to die, when she reach'd forth

Her hand with tapering fingers rosy-tipped
And touched me.   Then, once more myself, I saw
Her steeds, unbreath'd, draw up, and how there flashed
A sudden light o'er carven arch and door,
And sable towers and pillars glimmering fair;
And colonnades stretch'd darkling far away;
And in the distance, vistas dim were seen,
Like walks enchanted made for fairy feet;
And there stood Twilight like a lingering ray.
And like a fantary he went, and Eos,
A form of light, moved into shadowy halls,
And all the busy upper world was day.

And I awoke and turned my steps to where,
A mile away on the monotonous plain,
The hammers rang on shingle roofs, and grew
Each hour the "city" of a few weeks old.

A REVERIE.

My thoughts poor plummet deep I sink,
  But never bottom find,
And, rudder gone and compass lost,
  The sport of every wind,

Survey the veiled-up heavens in vain;
  No sun-gleam in the day,
And in the night never a star,
  E'en could I shape my way.

Like wild sea gulls my mind wheels on—
  A weary worthless chase,
And sometimes folds her jaded wing,
  And rests a little space.

No glimpse of blue the clouds glints through,
  Yet comes a sunny dream;
A boy bends o'er an old oak bridge
  And babbles to the stream.

At dusk the garden walls he scales,
  Himself and pockets fills,
Or holds a tryst with Mary Bate
  Beside old Lambert's Mills;

Or in the play ground 'mid a ring
  He fights with Charlie Brown,
One dreadful moment there they stand,
  The next and Brown is down.

The big boys lift them up and cry:
   " Now for another round !"
They wildly strike, then close again;
   This time he meets the ground.

A third time front to front they stand,
   Brown takes him 'neath the chin,
But soon gets into chancery,
   And so must e'en give in.

With claret, so we called it then,
   My sleeve shows many a stain,
But victor never prouder felt
   Upon the foughten plain.

The river fouls in flowing on,
   To taste its waves we shrink,
But at its source the stream is pure,
   And angels there might drink;

And pure that stream to which I fly
   From present thoughts appalling,
And liquid clear it strikes the ear,
   Like founts on Pindus falling.

Ah ! then whate'er the world's time,
   However dark the sky,
Refulgent suns of youth sublime
   Light up the inner eye:

Sweet tender memories full of sounds
   Of home, and fragrant days
All glad, and dewy lawns, and hounds,
   And games, and wholesome praise.

Bright morning trips with rosy smiles
   Across those ancient pine,
And in her glance the white rose glows,
   Two garden lakelets shine.

My dogs bound round with eager bark,
   And fain would force the will,
They wag their tails and gripe the hand,
   And look towards yonder hill,

Where well they know a hundred hares
   Through dewy brambles peep;
The hill is gained; old Gip gives cry;
   And puss flies up the steep.

A vigorous run, the quarry's won,
   I rest upon the ridge,
And watch the river roll below,
   The wain toil o'er the bridge,

The village white, the curling smoke,
   The old stone spire, the school,
The listening horse, the grazing kine,
   The fat geese in the pool.

And then across the fields for home,
   By hedges fresh and green,
Where berries oft invite to pause,
   And wild flowers bloom between.

Soon in that ancient antler'd hall
   My dogs jump and rejoice;
I hear the maids sing at their work,
   I hear my mother's voice;

She comes to know how fortune fared;
  I see her look so bright;
Her golden hair, her sweet blue eye,
  Her tiny figure slight.

The game I show, receive a kiss;
  Ah! who could dream the years
Would roll and roll, until one day
  That kiss would cause but tears?

Above dark woods of oak and elm,
  The placid moon shines clear;
A young man in a garden bower —
  He holds his breath to hear.

His eyes on fire, as tho' enraged,
  Survey the twinkling stars;
His heart beats like some wild thing caged
  Against its prison bars.

A glimpse of muslin—flash of feet,
  And eyes—red lips apart
In smiles.   He springs his love to greet;
  She's folded to his heart.

He kisses her; he pats her hair;
  One long perfervid kiss:
His life he'd wreak in kisses there,
  For life has naught like this.

But she must go — O yes she must —
  Another kiss and then —
Yes she must go to-morrow night,
  To-morrow in the glen.

Thus Fancy flying through the past
　　Flits now from that to this,
And present woe is all forgot
　　In unforgotten bliss.

On magic waves I'm borne away
　　To happier shores serene,
Where founts of joy forever play
　　'Mid fields for ever green.

And here at times a stronger spell
　　Upon my spirit falls,
I lie on banks of Asphodel
　　And tread Elysian halls,

While thronging round come shapes of light.
　　With eyes of temper'd fire;
The Muses nine, the Graces three,
　　Apollo with his lyre;

And fairer forms than e'er were feigned
　　On poets powerful scroll
And sweeter strains of rarer song,
　　Than e'er touch'd human soul.

The world is enter'd--comes the prose;
　　Man's falsehood, woman's wiles,
The plot of scoundrels o'er the wine,
　　The treachery masked in smiles.

The dream is gone—the river fades,
　　Those wooded heights are lost,
Once more upon a lonely sea
　　A lonely bark is tost.

THE CANADIAN YEAR.

The depths of infinite shade,
The soft green dusk of the glade,
With fiery fingers the frost had fret,
And dyed a myriad hue,
Making the forests temples of golden aisles:
The swooning rose forgot to bloom;
In fragrant graves slept violets blue;
And earlier shook her locks of jet
Night, with her subtle shadowy wiles,
Night, with her starry gloom,—
Before like suns which could not set,
Your eyes shone clear on mine,
Flushing the heart with feelings high,
Touching all life as thrills the sky,
When over cloudy pavements thunders rumble and roll;
Then flamed the faltering blood like wine,
And overflowed the soul.

Through wintery weeks, the sun above
Oceaned in blue, the frost below;
Through blustry hours, when fiercely drove
Winds razor-armed the drifting snow,
And peeled the face and pinched the ear,
And hurled the avalanche of fear
From roof-tops on the mufllered crowd;
The air one blinding cloud;
Through many a brisk and bracing day,

The sky wide summer as in June,
  The joyous sleighbells ringing tune
More blithe than aught musicians play;
  The pure snow gleaming white;
Men's eyes fulfilled of finer light,
Of finer tints the women's hair;
  Their cheeks aglow, and full and pink;
  The skaters sweeping through the rink,
Like swallows through the air:
We talked, and walked, and laughed and dreamed,
  And now snow-wreaths, auroral rays,
  The winter moon, day's blinding blaze,
  The merry bells, the skaters' grace
  Recall thy laugh, recall thy face,
As dazzling as it earliest beamed!

Love stirred in the frozen branches,
  And straight the world was crown'd with green,
And as a shipwright his trim craft launches,
Each bud put forth in a night its might,
  And the trees stood proud in summer sheen,
  Their foliage dense, a grateful screen
'Gainst the bold bright heat and the full fierce light.
Like cathedral windows the gardens glowed,
  Mirrors of light the broad lakes gleamed,
His cunning in song the robin showed,
  And the shore-lark swung on a branch and dreamed;
And boats were gliding, lover-laden,
  Over lakes and streams that will yet be known,
The boy in flannel, the blooming maiden
  In muslin white with a ribbon zone.

The chestnuts fell.   From their dull green sheaths
  With satin-white linings, the nuts burst free;
And as sun-down came, bright hazy wreaths
  The spirit of eve hung from tree to tree.
The weeks rolled on, the lush green fields
  Became billowy breadths of golden grain,
And all roots and fruits the kind earth yields
  Were piled on the labouring wain –
But you were by the cliff-barred white-crested sea,
  And I where the delicate pink of the prairie rose
    Amid rich coarse grasses hides,
Where the sunset's a boisterous pageantry,
  And the mornings the tenderest tints disclose,
  Where far from the shade and shelter of wood,
  The prairie hen rears her speckled brood,
    And the prairie wolf abides,
And lonely memory searching through
  Found no such stars in the orbèd past,
As the glad first greeting 'twixt me and you,
  And the sad, mad meeting which was our last.

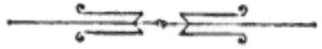

TO " BAY MI."

Lacking a good three years of seven,
Sunny-haired boy with eyes of heaven,
With everlasting ripple of laughter;
As yet no touch of worldly leaven
In thy frank soul. Oh! how you capture
All hearts, and drown in present joy
The cares which come from before and after,
Sunny-haired, blue-eyed, happy boy!

Running, jumping, never at rest,
　Now using one toy, now abusing another,
Caning your dearest friends in jest,
　Ruling father and sister and mother,
And bowing all wills to your high behest—
I could watch your movements all day long;
　Whether you laugh or whether you cry,
　Like a bird or a rill you enchain the eye,
And you fill the heart like a burst of song.

As pageants held in ruined towers
Will make the sad place glad once more,
As laughing waves on wreck-strewn shore,
As summer sunshine after showers,
You brighten up the weary heart,
And charm with sweet unconscious wiles,
So that the tears which still will start,
Before they fall are lost in smiles,
And you are folded to my breast,

And patted and caressed;
My hand runs through your golden hair,
The world is seen in hues of love,
There's not a cloud in heaven above,
    And all the earth is fair !
Scorn and hate—each evil passion flies
Before the beauty of your sinless eyes

You—best of preachers I have seen !
    You steal into the heart, bid flow
    The dried up streams of long ago,
    The farthest shores of memory glow
With fragrant flowers and tempering green.
So that this truth I more discern,
    If moral beauty we would wed,
    We must, as the Great Master said,
Of little children learn.

OTTAWA, April 17th, 1884.

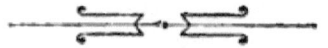

CHRISTMAS DAY AT OTTAWA.

(COMPOSED WHILE LOOKING AT THE CHAUDIÈRE FALLS FROM
THE PAVILION ON PARLIAMENT HILL.)

The broad snowy landscape, blue sky over-bending,
The river closed up, but the course of its trending
Apparent through woodland and mountain all bare;
   And glazing and gilding, and buttress and building,
And tower and turret, a-gleam in the glare
   Of a sun, of a brightness complete and unyielding,
And Hull like a camp, and the lumber like war tents;
The roar of the Chaudière – the smoke of its torments
Flung high in the clear frosty air, like the breath
Of some monster Titanic, in torture of death.

And the sleigh bells are singing, and jingling, are flinging
   Their music of gladness through resonant air,
And folk, drest *en fête*, wend where church bells are ringing,
   And man kneels to heaven and proffers his prayer;
Where through arches of green the deep organ-note rolls,
   And the cross is bedeck'd with the spoil of the trees,
And legends of mercy, from fanciful scrolls,
   Breathe hope to the sin-laden crowd on its knees.
But the sun's a shekinah, the white snow an altar,
And whose faith, 'mid such scene, on this day, dares to falter?
Trade's bustle is hushed, and great Nature calls
The soul to its God by the voice of those falls.

And those waters which howl o'er the bleak rocks forever,
   Now slow to the sea 'neath the ice silent roll,
Like some life full of purpose, but shrouded endeavour,
   That spurns acclaim, yet wins on to the goal;
Like God's life in Christ— can the mind there find rest?
   A manger, a maiden, a babe newly born!—
Can that tiny hand which soft presses the breast,
   Be his who rules oceans and reins in the storm?
His the hand who let loose those wild waves in their might,
And softened their terror with sweet rainbow light?
Do not fear   have but faith—and hark! how he calls
The soul to his soul thro' the sound of those falls.

O Father and source of whatever is fair!
   Fill my soul with such strength as to nature belongs.
The cataract's force as it leaps from its lair,
   The sweetness of Summer and Summer birds' songs;
A will like a law to no passion e'er bending,
   A heart that respends but to noble desires,
And thoughts wing'd with light'ning of Heaven's own lending,
   And a fancy illumin'd with Heaven's own fires.
On this bright Xmas Day, which annihilates care,
In Christ's name I offer this confident prayer,
And, with heart that nor future nor present appals,
Thy blessing I hear in the boom of those falls.

PARTED.

The cold, cruel gods who for ever
   Sway men's destinies, doomed we should meet.
The cold, cruel gods !– who now sever
   Two wild hearts which bound but to greet;
And then bound as the lark from his low bed,
   And sing as he sings when on high,
When the sun o'er the earth hath his glow shed,
   And his splendour is broad in the sky.

The flush of thy cheek was as morning,
   As her star, the sweet light in thine eyes.
To a heart wrapt in darkness deforming,
   And tost in a tempest of sighs;
And I dreamed in a sleep, sweet to sadness,
   As thy red lips in fancy I prest,
That that heart should beat high with noon's gladness,
   And should bask in the beams of the west.

But lo ! ere the day-spring is dewless,
   Ere the shrill lark's loud matin is o'er,
I look for thy form, but 'tis viewless,
   For thy voice, but I hear it no more;
And Night with the boom of her beetles,
   Dethrones Day with the songs of her birds,
There are death knells from shadowy steeples,
   And wailings too wild for all words;

And I roam like some soul banned from blessing,
  Amid scenes where joy's cup used o'er-brim,
And bemocked of a phantom caressing,
  And the ghost of a conjugal hymn;
There's a night in my heart past fate's scorning,
  Since above it no morrow shall rise,
For the flush of thy cheek was my morning,
  My day star, the light in thine eyes.

GOOD NIGHT.

(WRITTEN AT WINNIPEG, FEB., 1879, ON READING A LETTER
IN WHICH THE WRITER SAID: "ICH DENKE IMMER
AN DICH.")

Good night! rest craves this wearied brain,
    And rest these eyes of mine;
But lo! they're wide awake again,
    And looking into thine.

Thy glance sincere my fancy takes,
    And every sense it thrills,
And o'er my heart thy calm smile breaks,
    Like morning o'er the hills.

The wintry night, a summer light,
    At thy approach doth show,
The raptured stars shine yet more bright,
    More pure those banks of snow.

O little room! O shabby room!
    That'st heard my sacred vow,
In splendours veil thy dingy gloom,
    She's thinking of me now!

I know it! By yon stars which roll
    Bright sister lamps apart!
The soul may strike thro' space to soul;
    Heart telephone to heart.

O happy pain! Conflicting fate!
    To love what's all divine,
And yet to have no offering great,
    To lay upon her shrine.

"Away such thoughts! 'tis vain to grieve
    At smallness of my store,
For had I empire's dower to give,
    I still would give thee more.

And had I more than empire's dower,
    Still more I'd fain bestow,
Great Jove might lend me all his power,
    Yet my demands would grow.

Beyond the verge of mortal bounds
    My heart's desires expand,
Far—far—through wide eternal rounds,
    I'd lead thee by the hand.

But that my bliss thy bliss could mar,
    Did God this hour me show,
I'd face cold ways which know no star,
    I'd dry my tears and go.

For may my years stand all accurst,
    My flag fall in the strife,
If I don't rate thy peace as first,
    And love thee more than life.

Good night! thou'rt here—my heart throbs vouch;
    Thy heart too sure must leap;
Sweet! bend thee o'er my wintry couch,
    And kiss these eyes to sleep.

A SONG.

April, September,
    December, July,
This year's love who'll remember,
    When next year's sun is high ?
But some hearts don't falter
    As passing suns set,
And tho' thou'lt surely alter
    I'll cling to thee yet.
O sweet ! how sweet we should have met !
O sweet ! how sad I can't forget.

My vow I have broken
    This heart thus let free,
And the passion outspoken
    I cherish for thee.
Ah ! my years may grow dreary
    And darker than jet,
And this soul still more weary
    But I'll think of thee yet.
O sweet ! how sweet we should have met !
O sweet ! how sad I can't forget !

The courage is shaken
   That bowed to no blast,
And time has o'ertaken
   My spirit at last.
But autumn may mellow,
   The branch become sere,
The winter winds bellow
   But thou'lt still be dear.
O sweet! how sweet we should have met!
O sweet! how sad I can't forget!

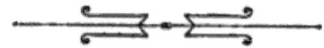

BY THE SEA—A DREAM.

Where the wild sea rolls up the sultry sand,
    Methought we met ;
I marked the movements of the billows grand,
    And eyes of jet.

On days of calm upon its placid breast,
    Watch'd the sunlight :
And then my glance upon thy face would rest,
    More calm, more bright.

When rose the moon above the slumberous sea,
    I gazed, the while
Her sweet light rain'd enchantment, then on thee
    I look'd ; thy smile

Was sweeter than those magic beams ; my breath
    Became a sigh.
Ah ! if in such an hour should come dread death,
    'Twere sweet to die !

And then again, heart-glad, my laugh would break
    As stirr'd by wine,
Or joyful news, to know that I could take
    Thy hand in mine,

And feel I was not all unprized by thee,
    To whom my soul
Turn'd strong, as turns the full stream to the sea,
    The needle to the pole.

A FEW BRIEF HOURS—HOW QUICK THEY FLY.

A few brief hours—how quick they fly—
   Our barks together bore.
Away! black clouds begrime the sky,
   Go seek the safer shore.

For round my boat will billows foam,
   Ahead will breakers roll.
Away! who fain with me would roam
   Must bear no shrinking soul.

I do not blame—I don't complain,
   You should lie close and warm,
For me, I love the hurricane,
   Am kindred with the storm.

Because my star's obscured from view,
   Doubt fills your faltering breast ;
But my heart's needle still points true ;
   To God I leave the rest.

Her sail fades o'er the whitening wave,
   She sights her bowers of ease,
But round me soon will storms rave,
   And rise great angry seas.

The thunders crash —the lightnings flare—
   The wild surge sweeps each mast—
But tho' my keel should plough the air,
   I'll gain the goal at last.

Away! who loves may follow me.
   Hark to the canvas strain!
Away! to win the argosy
   That plows the distant main!

A STAR.

A star—a star upon the sea,
A star so far so cold to me.
A star on snowy landscape bold,
A star more near, a star less cold.
What could it mean that star for me
That once I saw down by the sea?

What may it bode that star so bright,
That glimmers 'cross the crusty white?
I cannot tell: I only know,
It sweetly shines across the snow.

It may be but a passing gleam
Upon my life's sad-flowing stream;
It may be Destiny's own glow
That beckons me across the snow.

I do not know. I only feel
Its influence thro' my bosom steal,
And, as by magic, o'er me throw
A sense of Summer spite of snow.

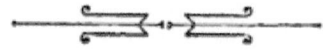

FLOWERS.

Sweeter than flowers, tenderer than dawns of June
   Bedewed, is young and lovely womanhood,
   When in her bosom vibrates every good,
And pity, truth and virtue make one perfect tune.

As pure as these I hoped that life would be,
   But like a dream the fond hope disappears,
   A glimmering ghost down vistas of dark years,
And heart bereaved I fly from thought to thee.

NUMBERS.

A few words all surcharged with deepest heart—
   And all the fun and frolic die away.
    I read your letters—all their charming play
Of wit but causes bitter tears to start.

Talk not of numbers—these are counted o'er,
   And bear proportion. In my reckoning now
    Is none like thee. From chin to dark-crown'd brow,
Thy face—love's cameo carved in memory's core.

Thy liquid laughter haunts like old world song,
   And thro' my all too darkened days thy smiles,
    Like sudden sunbeams in old dusky aisles,
Dispelling gloom, dispersing thoughts of wrong.

And come what may—you first and last must be;
   The star that lingers when the rest have set;
    A light of joy I never can forget;
A power that sways around me like the sea.

RECONCILED.

O God! To see thee weep
 And dare not kiss
The tear, the bursting tear away.
 My love! my life! my soul!
  My highest bliss
Were near thee ever more to stay,
 To stay for ever more.

But now a gulf yawns wide
 Between us two;
The sun is gone, nor star
 Illumes the dark; my peace
  Is gone, and you
Stand yonder —sad and cold and far—
 Far, far for ever more.

But lift thy drooping lids
 And light the dark
Expanse; but smile though sad twill bridge
 The gulf with joy, and speak
  One word!—the lark
Sings on the gleaming ridge
 Of dawn! 'Tis night no more.

FAREWELL.

All the sorest pangs that ever
  Preyed within my bosom's cell,
Were as nothing to the sorrow
  Of our first and last farewell.

Hope was strong; but hope is blighted;
  Her once bright eyes dimm'd with tears;
And the shadow of her sorrow
  Darkens o'er the coming years.

For tho' lighter loves have loiter'd
  Round the portal—by the wall—
Thine alone hath ever enter'd
  In the holiest of all.

No rapt devotee adoring
  At some saint's ascetic shrine,
Needs to cherish feelings holier
  Than for thee were ever mine;

And perhaps here is the secret
  That the spell has been so strong,
That you first woke noble feelings
  That had slept too sound and long,

And thus taught the soul to listen
  Glad, for graver tones and sweet,
Than the wanton Circean dirges
  Wild, that swell down passion's street;

And a dawn of nobler doing
  Rose before the jaded eyes,
And a star of purer promise
  Sparkled in serener skies;

And the long long hidden fountains,
  Of a noble boyhood's dreams,
Broke their subterranean fetters,
  Filled the desert heart with streams.

Ah my God! what ground for marvel,
  If belief grew strong each hour,
That you came as sent by heaven,
  To give thought and life new power?

But tho' past the hope of winning
  Constant strength from constancy,
Yet will, in the heart's sad gloaming,
  Live refracted rays of thee.

Aye, and tho' I take as final,
  This our fatal last farewell,
Thoughts now sweet, now sad, will quicken,
  Feelings deep and tender swell,

When the wilful memory wanders
  Wild, as wander oft she will,
Ghosts of hopes from burial calling,
  Hopes that you alone could kill.

But farewell ! my heart is breaking,
   Love, resolve may render less,
But that morning dawns in darkness,
   I released from tenderness.

So farewell ! the poor heart lingers
   Near her dead—hangs o'er the bier :
" Draw her thence ; let go the funeral ;
   She is but a hinderance here."

And the dead from sight is buried ;
   Whips crack loud ; men go their ways ;
But the mourner, in her chamber,
   Weeps alone the weary days.

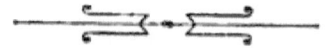

SINCE FIRST O'ER ALBUM VERSE I GROANED.

Since first o'er Album verse I groaned,
　　What years have passed me by !
'Twas hard to think the girl who owned
　　That foolish book could die.

But strange to say that die she did ;
　　No fish escapes death's hook ;
And stranger still, her memory slid
　　Quite out of memory's book.

And tho' I love you very much,
　　And mine is love in sooth,
Ne'er credit me, my love is such
　　As will defy Time's tooth.

To please thee, I'd resign my breath,
　　Or more — I'd write a rhyme ;
But tho' my love is strong as **Death**,
　　It is not strong as Time.

THE LANDLADY'S DAUGHTER.

Other poets meet
  Their mistress in a garden,
Watering happy flowers,
  Drest like Dolly Varden;
Mine's a happier fate,
  Makes every hour so tender,
For Jennie cleans the grate
  And toilets up the fender.

O, my anguish dire,
  I'm sadder than Lord Lovell,
When I see her coax the fire,
  And cuddle the old shovel;
My heart is full of wrongs,
  That I never spoke her,
I'm jealous of the tongs,
  I hate that rakish poker.

O, what joys must rest,
  Where this hand would falter!
Blest rose upon her breast,
  Thrice blest the beaded halter.
I would be that rose,
  And tho' dry as rushes,
My sap should gather power,
  My leaves bloom back her blushes;

And eke that beaded chain,
  Gods! how each bead would quiver,
When love shot through a vein,
  Like sunlight through a river!

Her mother ruled the house,
  And acted small and shabby,
She made me play the mouse,
  While she played the old tabby.
Never once a tasty dish,
  But all things one would tire on,
She gave me ancient fish,
  And beef steak hard as iron

Once I grew quite red,
  Th' untouched beef steak brought her,
She tost her handsome head:
  " 'Twas purchased by my daughter.'
I just touched Jennie's slender
  Waist, and said: " Enough.
But never aught so tender
  Purchased aught so tough."

—— ✕ · · ·

AUGUSTA.

We met, how blithe my laughter rang,
    And years fared forth in sparkling billows,
And through the pearls and corals sang,
    And flashed beneath your eyelids' willows.

I went into the night, each star
    Was bright as when it glowed on Adam;
I struck a match — lit my cigar,
    And said: "So, so, I'll flirt with Madam."

And flirt we did, nor did I fear
    The witchery of those glancing eyes,
Would darken all I then held dear,
    Make light all things I ought to prize;

My pulse was high, my heart was gay,
    My purpose strong 'gainst all fate hurled;
But now, old hopes no longer stay,
    And you could lure me round the world.

———— ✕ ————

TO KINKOMETTA THE QUADROON.

O Tinkometta - fair quadroon,
  Soon, soon, I leave your wilds of snow,
Your prattling ways I'll lose too soon,
  Then take my blessing ere I go.
Four bloods within your being meet,
  Four influences blend,
The English give their red rose sweet,
  The Scotch their thistle lend:
In beauty and in strength array'd
  Its motto— how express it?
Missing a word 'twill suit a maid:
  Nemo me lacessit.
Wit's sparkle, all that's linked with grace,
  The sound of song and dance,
From many a trellised viny place—
  These are the gifts of France.
Thy Indian blood should riches bring
  From prairie and from brake,
The forest glade, the eagle's wing,
  The lonely glimmering lake:
The white falls startling solitude,
  Long months of winter's reign,
The sun-god in his morning mood,
  Or setting thwart the plain.

Thus whatsoe'er's romantic—wild—
   Is linked with culture high ;
You're now a fascinating child,
   A woman by-and-bye ;
And if you'll take a bard's advice,
   You'll watch o'er all you feel,
And guard your heart—that pearl of price--
   Lest some boy should it steal ;
For tho' mythology is grey,
   And Grecian gods rise never,
Yet trust me, love is love to-day,
   And Cupid's spry as ever.
Four bloods within your being meet,
   Four influences blend,
May every grace your young life greet,
   Peace crown its happy end.

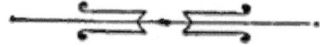

VALENTINE.

A Flora's head; from eyes a shower
    Of starlight over face and figure,
And in the mouth a sense of power,
    And in the step a note of vigour.

Hair, blacker than the murkiest night:
    No pads, no friz—lynx-eyes may scan it;
The forehead, a piece of lunar light,
    Cut by an archway on white granite.

The column'd neck—but I must pause;
    My senses reel—what if I lose 'em!
Old Hogarth's line—sweet beauty's laws
    Are folded in that ample bosom.

A form—no angel's—rather hers
    Who came with Neptune's sunny spray lit,
We'd swear, or else my judgment errs,
    If you had wings to fly away with.

We met, once in the busy street,
    And once when dancing ruled the season;
We did not dance—but yet your feet
    Bore me along in spite of reason.

And so I sit to-day and weave
    This little wreath of careless rhyming,
And half I joy, and half I grieve,
    To know my name's beyond divining.

As one might sing to some sweet star
   Upon the young night's forehead glowing,
I sing to you, so near—so far—
   Hold on your radiant course unknowing.

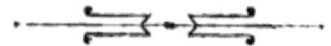

TO MRS. CORBETT.

In other days when love was king,
　Betimes I learned to woo,
And whoso asked me then to sing,
　Could have a stave or two.

But now my Muse is lumpish grown,
　And laughs at Cupid's token,
And my poor heart—'tis but a stone,
　So hard—though often broken.

Thus as I pondered deep to-day,
　And for invention panted,
My Muse grew bright as any fay,
　Enchanting and enchanted !

And from her lips such music stole,
　As never on this orb yet
Was heard, I cried : " My Muse ! my soul !"
　My Muse ! 'Twas Mrs. Corbett.

TO G —

Of ladies gay, in verses brief,
  I've sung and ta'en the early rose,
And asked of every dewy leaf,
  What could its tender tints disclose
More fair than those which, ruby bright,
  Glowed on young cheeks, now red now fainter,
Until they merged in lily white,
  Which shamed the snow, defied the painter.

But when I fain would sing of thee,
  In vain my midnight lamp I burn,
Nor rose, nor wild anemone
  Will serve my dainty Muse's turn;
She spreads her airy wings afar,
  And bathes in stellar dews her crest,
And then you glow that loveliest star
  Which diamonds young Aurora's breast.

A PHOTOGRAPH.

A photograph adorns my room
   Two sweet young faces there,
Thank God, no tyrant speaks my doom –
   To say which is more fair—

The evening star is sweet to see,
   The morning star is bright,
But what conclave could e'er agree
   Which gives the purer light ?

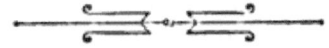

I ASKED SWEET LOVE.

I asked sweet love,
  Where we should meet,
    And greet,
Secure from slips?
On earth beneath, in heaven above?
He answer'd quick with quivering wings.
  That perfumed zephyrs stirr'd around,
All crisp with spray from springs
    Of tears,
  Deep laid in rapture's heart profound,
    Long gathered in immemorial years:
" We'd meet, sir, on your lady's lips."

THE YOUNG BRIDE.

We three talk'd of her yesterday;
　　Her father and her mother,
And he who writes this little lay,
　　In heart a kind of brother.
Her gentle beauty, art had placed
　　Upon the shelf before us,
And all the gifts her soul that graced,
　　Like summer lights play'd o'er us.

We thought we saw her there the while,
　　Recall'd each playful saying,
The archness in the mouth's sweet smile,
　　The humour round it playing;
The universal love that met
　　Her kind heart outward going,
The cheerfulness which never set,
　　The charity ever-flowing.

How many a time while music roll'd,
　　And twang'd the saucy fiddle,
We two sat on the stair, and told
　　A story or a riddle;
Or laughed—no scornful laugh—at those
　　Who bill'd and coo'd around us;
The music stopp'd—then up we rose,
　　The slight bond burst that bound us.

Oh! all her gracious ways that day
  As we three talk'd together,
Came like the smell of new-mown hay,
  Or of the blossom'd heather,
Upon the hearts of those three friends:
  Two knew her all her past years,
While he who here a mourner bends,
  But knew her these few last years.

But, who that knew her, months or years,
  Could hear that death had taken
So sweet a soul, nor let hot tears
  Show that his soul was shaken?
The spouseless spouse! Let fall the veil!
  Hush! hush! That ground's too holy!
O Youth! O Death! O tragic tale!
  Young widower bending lowly!

To think of yesterday, and all
  The gladsome memories swelling,
And now for that young life the pall,
  The mournful church-bell knelling!
Toll out sad notes, but also sweet;
  Let hope our sorrow leaven;
She is not dead; tho' here we meet
  No more: we'll meet in Heaven.

THE PRAYER.

Tell me did he hear thee maiden ?
  Did he grant thy gentle prayer ?
Does he rest the heavy laden ?
  Is there balm for wounding there ?

Beyond voids no science bridges,
  Beyond suns no glass can sight,
Beyond calm eternal ridges,
  Casting shadows infinite,

Where he dwells in vast seclusion,
  Which not fancy's wing can reach,
Does he heed the fond illusion,
  That he recks man's feeble speech ?

Say, did bright-robed angels flutter
  O'er thy young form bending there ?
Did some voice mysterious utter,
  Sure responses to thy prayer?

          *   *   *   *

Angels bright-robed may have flutter'd
  O'er me bowed in sorrow there,
But no voice mysterious utter'd
  Aught responsive to my prayer.

Only in my heart I felt where
   Softly Jesus gently stirred,
And around me as I knelt there.
   All the effluence of the Word.

Yes, Lord ! coarse sense failed to hear thee.
  Sense made dull by sin's black wine,
Yet my God I knew thee near me.
   And my spirit touched by thine.

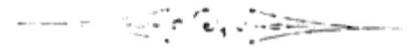

MASKS AND FACES.

The features of the fairest face
   Are little more than signs.
And but of ugliness the mask,
If they don't find their highest task,
In telling of a higher grace
   That in the soul's face shines.

Bright eyes of blue, or grey, or jet,
   Or lovelier still thine own,
Grow dim as chambers of the night,
If they're not fed with living light.
A mental sun which cannot set,
   Till life's red leaves are blown.

And when those leaves are scatter'd wide,
   The frost-bit branches sere,
The garden one cold wint'ry scene.
The abounding rose but what has been,
The lily fair but what has died,
   And all is bleak and drear ;

O ! in that desert hour—what then ?
   Let beauty mourn; that glass,
Which of its lot could one day brag,
But renders back a wrinkled hag ;
   Let genius know for other men
   His wand was made and pass.

But whither ! O the cruel gods
  Whose silent wheels sweep past !
Rest ! rest brave heart—the shadows grow,
And cold and colder lies the snow,
And soft and softer press the sods,
  And you have peace at last.

What matters now vile Slander's hissing ?
  The venom'd deadly dart !
That heads grew drunk to gaze on forms,!
Which since have proved cold joints for worms ?
That lips were red for kissing,
  That heart beat wild for heart ?

What thoughts built up the soul, what made
  The music of the breast —
This, this alone concerns you now,
And Beauty's smile, and Fame's large brow
Are but as wiles of some wild jade,
  Whose smile's a common pest.

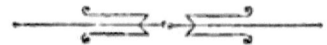

HYGIEA.

O shining mistress of the pure and strong!
  Crown'd with May blossoms, sun-lit thy blue eye –
Cans't thou forgive my wanderings, oft and long,
  From thy firm bosom where the bold may lie,
  Nor fear the guilty pinion hovering nigh?

Fill, fill the wine cup!   Drink, drink fathoms deep!
  Crown you with garlands, roses dewed with wine?
Hence carking care?   Be banished gentle sleep!
  Let Revel dance, gay wit's glad lightnings shine,
  And laughter grow more loud with night's decline.

The sun is up; the perfumed landscape glows;
  The streams go silvering thro' the meadows green:
The golden mist o'er all things glory throws,
  A thousand flowers breathe incense round their queen
  Whose white and red make mock of beauty's sheen.

Ah! my blithe reveller, where now art thou!
  Thy beaming eye, quick wit, wild laughter's swell!
That eye is dull, dark gloom nods on thy brow,
  Thy heart sways sadly, thy hot brain's a hell,
  And e'en the wine has lost its quick'ning spell.

O shining mistress of the pure and free!
  No more I'll quit thy strong inspiring hand,
Nor shun to joy with thee on life's great sea,
  Whereon we'll sail, nor fear the fateful strand,
  Where mid blanch'd bones the chanting Sirens stand.

THE CHARITABLE NIGHT SHIRT.

I once went far to see
  Some maids with whom I might flirt;
They were bent on charity,
  And proposed to make a night shirt,

For the good of some good cause,
  Orphans or such weak chickens;
I'd have ordered without pause,
  If the cause were at the dickens.

I called again —to know
  Of that work my ears were itchin',
When the ladies, quite aglow,
  Told me all about the stitchin'.

How 'twas cut out by one,
  Its full length undiminished,
How the gussets they were done,
  And how the whole was finished.

The coals were waxing low,
  And fainter the flames' flashes;
Like my hot youth's fervid glow,
  What was once fire now was ashes.

I began to scratch my head,
  Like some posed and puzzled varmint—
And I thought, I'll go to bed,
  And try on the new garment.

Scarce got beneath the clothes,
  My hand beneath my head, sir,
Fixed for a night's repose —
  When I sprang clean out of bed, sir.

What was wrong? O patience please—
  Every fibre was a-twitchin';
Those gussets stung like bees,
  And like wasps the dainty stitchin'.

To pull it off I tried,
  But it hugg'd me close, oppressive;
And, while struggling, I espied
  A sweet face most expressive;

And a form! - I think, I swore
  I ne'er saw aught so splendid —
She but said: "You'll sleep no more,
  Your nights of rest are ended."

And she smiled — gods! how she smiled!
  And how her black eyes glistened!
From my pangs I was beguiled,
  As to that voice I listened.

I stooped to kiss her hand,
  White as milk fresh from a dairy,
She drew back with curtsy bland,
  And then vanish'd like a fairy.

And now I never sleep,
  And I'm tortur'd as I told, sir,
And I think I sometimes weep,
  With longing to behold her;

But from her I'm exiled,
   That maid with face bewitchin';
And the gussets drive me wild,
   And I'm madden'd by the stitchin'.

AN IRISH FAIR.

SUGGESTED BY THE PEASANTS' SONG IN "FAUST."

Now Paddy to the dancing flew.
His shirt was clean, his necktie new.
  And Peggy's gown and face were beaming;
Beneath the canvas every spark
Was gay as dewy morning's lark,
      Yukheh ! Yukheh !
      Yukheizah ? heizah ! heh !
The fiddle sticks were screaming.

And Phelim sidled up to Proo,
And round her waist his arm drew,
  The spalpeen sure was ravin':
The modest colleen jumped aside,
Half crimson with offended pride,
      Yukheh ! Yukheh !
      Yukheizah ! heizah ! heh !
Now don't be misbehavin'.

But at his smile offence takes flight,
They dance to left, they dance to right,
  Their hands their hips are clutching;
They grow quite red, they grow quite warm,
Then on they wander arm in arm,
      Yukheh ! Yukheh !
      Yukheizah ! heizah ! heh !
'Neath the trees their lips are touching.

Come, come, sir, be not quite so bold,
Or you shall find that I can scold,
   This is the way of men's betrayin';
He comes the blarney, utters vows,
   And on they roam 'neath blossomed boughs,
      Yukheh ! Yukheh !
      Yukheizah ! heizah ! heh !
And far from crowds the two are straying.

THE ROBIN AND THE WORM.

Time —the Queen's Birthday; Place —the hill,
I watch'd a robin ply his bill.
To see him operate I turned
From visions half-divine.   I spurned
The sprayed white thunder of the falls,
The mountains robed in misty palls,
Quite Turneresque—that made them seem
Like things which rise up in a dream;
The circles of foam on the river's breast
Hurrying on to its Ocean rest;
The bowery green o'er the Lover's Walk;
A curious, delicious, fortuitous talk
With a pretty girl, drest in print;
No critic had said: "There's nothing in't."
Like May with apple blossoms crown'd,
She was tall and fresh and slim and round;
Nor rose, nor rose bud—but just between:
The Venus de Milo at seventeen.
From her dainty hat—past the full white neck
Down to her waist—like a mountain beck—
Fell a stream of dark brown hair.
She had moreover a certain air
Of being a saint.   She carried a missal,
And looked as demure as a Pauline epistle.
I talked of the greyish tint of the skies,
But thought of the tint of her deep blue eyes.

I carelessly said: "The City of Hull
Looks empty of life;"— But my heart was full.
I noted the youth on her cheeks that shone,
And sighed to think my youth was gone.
I marked the cross on her heaving breast,
The emblem of suffering in beautiful rest.
Years ago in old St. Ouen,
The finest church in Norman Rouen,
I used to meet a girl like this;
In the church we'd pray and outside we'd kiss.
She was deeply concern'd for my future state;
I was absorbed in a nearer date.
We visited the churches old and quaint,
And paused at the shrine of many a saint.
One day when leaving St. Maclou I told her,
For me to love her, and to behold her,
Were one and the same: she blushed and said
Nothing whatever, but hung her head.
We met so often! I drank her smiles,
While the organ roll'd thro' the lonely aisles,
In hours of practice, when the artist's hand
Made every nook of the building grand
Tremble with sonorous harmony,
Now sweet as streams and now strong as the sea.
I saw her last behind the grill
Of a convent.

                    Now for that robin's bill.
He moved about the level green,
As stately as some youthful queen,
Or some sweet dame at Rideau Hall,
Who with His "Ex" leads off the ball.

He'd now retire, and now advance,
You'd think he practised some old dance.
At length he stood straight on the lawn,
And moved his head just like Sir John.

As the old Statesman eyes a paper,
Prepar'd by Blake to make him caper,
The robin eyed an opening where
A worm enjoyed the morning air.
" The question is shall *this bill* pass ?"
He said, and drove it in the grass.
He drew it back; the prize was won.
Said I: " That's not unlike Sir John."
He tugged, and pulled, and strained about,
And now he had nine inches out,
But still the twelve-inch worm profound,
Like bold debater held his ground.

The robin tugg'd and tugg'd; leaned back;
I thought his little thighs would crack.
A long, long pull, and I could see,
Like some young fool of high degree,
The worm was done for—being free.
Said I: " The way you've drawn your worm,
Is not unlike the Premier's form."

But here it seems the likeness ends.
If of the robin's foes or friends
I cannot say, but can avow,
·A little bird, from neighbouring bough,
Had watch'd the robin at his toil.
Silent he watch'd, nor did he spoil,

By a distracting note, the will
With which that robin plied his bill.

But when the arduous job was over,
He darted quickly from his cover,
And, without flutter of wings or pause,
He took the worm from out the jaws
Of the tired robin, who look'd dazed,
And stood a moment quite amazed,
Then slowly, sadly flew away,
Said I: " Ah *that's* not like John A."

But 'tis like many a mother's son;
We work, we strive; the prize is won ;
But when we come to claim the promise,
Some Jacob's ta'en the blessing from us.
The rythmic toiler earns his pay,
Which watchful cunning bears away.

From musing thus, I turn'd to see
    A fellow, who'd been making a bobbin,
Had taken my girl, and treated me,
    As the sparrow had treated the robin.

Ottawa, May 28th, 1884.

REGINA.*

Verses supposed to be recited on Victoria Street, in the year of the
City A. U. C. 22.

A pleasant city on a boundless plain,

Around rich land where peace and plenty reign;

A legal camp, the province wisdom's home,

A rich cathedral, learning's splendid dome;

A teeming mart, wide streets, broad squares, bright flowers.

A marble figure whence a fountain showers --

What city's this? A gentle princess, famed

For happy genius, it Regina named.

Its youth—(though born beneath a happy star)-

Was stormy, and each cur, from near and far,

Bark'd at the town; each ribald loudly talked,

Hirelings—projectors whose vile plans were balked.

They lied, they swore; loud was the ceaseless bray;

---

* The Winnipeg *Times* of January 3rd, 1884, had a poem headed
"Pile of Bones" by Futuro.

> "What mounds are those, carefully ploughed around?
> Some hunters' graves or Indian burial ground?
> Not so, my friend—some twenty years gone by,
> A town sprang up right here where you and I
> Now stand, which first as Pile of Bones was known."

And the writer went on to abuse the water, etc. At the time one of
the foremost writers in Canada was editing the *Times*, and was supposed to have penned the verses. I did not think them worth answering, but on entering a store on Broad Street, a gentleman suggested I
should answer them. I thereupon took up a pen and wrote the above
impromptu. One of the prophecies is fulfilled—but I hope the *Free
Press* and *Sun* may long flourish, even though they should continue
to be my bitter enemies.

Reginans smiled— Regina held her way,
The while traducers perished one by one.
And fate o'ertook each guilty mother's son.
Failing to bleed the tenderfoot, they bled
Themselves, or like their sires by hempen thread
Expired; and Winnipeg the city where
They lived and died, soon perished like a pear
That had the yellows.   Long the *Times* is dead;
The *Sun* has set; the *Free Press'* days are fled;
The lot of one wild scribbler stands alone;
The gods in anger turned him into stone,
And by an irony Ned called "divilish quare,"
Made him a fountain in Regina's square,
And there he stands— no wonder you're amused —
Spouting the water he so oft abused.

IN MEMORY OF A DINNER.

ADDRESSED TO THE LATE HON. J. B. PLUMB.

In other days round classic boards, I met
    With those whose young brows bore the laurel, pure
    From stain.   Talking of art and strong to endure
All things, we felt youth's star could never set.
The wine I spurn now like an anchoret,
    But oft from out the past I fain would lure
    The joyous wit, the impromptu portraiture,
The high philosophies which haunt me yet.

Fresh as those you gave us for a whet,
    Apicius sent cool bivalves to his friend
    In Parthia.   Many millions would he spend
On feasts colossal: but I'd make a bet
Than yours a choicer did he never get,
    And higher our young wits did ne'er ascend.

Ottawa, March 7th, 1884.

FRIENDSHIP.

Sweeet is the moon above old English trees,
  And sweet her light on dewy velvet lawns,
  And sweet her pallid shade in purple dawns,
And passing sweet her sheen on languid seas.
O'er sleeping kine on broad-extending leas,
  Dispersèd o'er the darkling green like pawns,
  Her light is sweet, and sweet when deep down yawns
The abyss, or whitens far wide prairies.

So friendship whereso'er we go is sweet;
  Whate'er of loss or triumph we may share;
  Whatever we endure, or do, or dare;
Nor can fate all be dark, if round our feet
  Its rays are shed; however 'mersed in care,
Beauty and Peace amid life's shadows meet.

TO E——

Historic lights athwart thy brow are cast;
   And while I gaze on thee, from night's profound,
   Bright forms, starry crown'd, come crowding round,
Their lucid outlines gleaming thro' the past.
'Twas with such eyes, the sorceress of Nile
   Ambition charmed to rest in Cæsar's heart,
   And if Scotch Mary, playing foulest part,
Subdued men's reason, 'twas with such a smile.

See that thy beauty be no fatal dower,
   Nor dull the heart, nor deaden the swift mind—
Beauty,—not certain for a single hour, —
   The dazzling bird of youth no cord can bind:
To-day his luring lithe enchantments shower
Divinity; to-morrow he's far down the mocking wind.

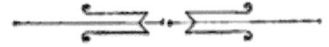

SIR JOHN MACDONALD, G. C. B.

COMPOSED IN THE OPERA HOUSE, TORONTO, DEC. 17, 1884.

The child of love and power and fame you came,
    An Empire's sunshine on your classic brow;
You came to meet a people's loud acclaim—
    The mighty future's murmur 'gainst the now:
And when that tide shall rise, with myriad sound,
    Bearing imperial hopes upon its breast,
Laving full many a margent city-crown'd,
    Reflecting many a mountain's airy crest;
Then, like some beacon-bearing headland, you
Shall tower on high, far seen across the blue,
To you, thro' lapsing years, shall turn the eyes
    Of those who fain would read the statesman's chart,
And learn, when torrents roar and tempests rise,
    To steer with wary hand and play a patriot's part.

LADY MACDONALD.

And now as fair a task, for I would sing
　　Of one whose purpose does not falter; one
Whose name with his shall down the centuries ring,
　　And grow more bright with each recurring sun.
Ah ! dearer far than star a queen can dower,
　　And dearer than the people's loud acclaim,
A noble woman's welcome, and the power
　　Her touch can give, whose life is void of blame.

We build men statutes; did but Justice speak,
　　She'd say: Do likewise for those gentler lives,
Who hid away from public gaze, but seek
　　The selfless guerdon won by faithful wives—
To do all love can do, all patience can,
And be the day-star of the work-worn, weary man.

A CHRISTMAS CARD.

The snowy waste all wild and wide.
  The blizzard bellows on its way.
  I see this card--the world's all May,
And you are sitting by my side.
This heart was ice an hour ago,
Now all the springs of feeling flow,
As 'mid the dance I see you glide,
  While gay waltz music fills the air;
  Or 'neath the moon—a happy pair—
We walk, nor care what may betide.
My heart swells glad with vanished bliss,
  All, all before my fancy rise—
  Your low sweet voice--your violet eyes—
Your lips,—your thrice perfervid kiss.

ABSENT.

Fair as the beauteous morning's golden beam
   That glowing steals o'er dewy perfum'd flowers;
You come and linger in sad fancy's dream,
   And happy pain beguiles the tortur'd hours,
I think you present— then my heart is glad;
   I know you absent—then I fain would fly
To where you are—but must not—so I'm sad—
   And rapture dies; my soothest song's a sigh.

The chains of love are round me; I must love;
   I cannot if I would, I would not free
   Myself from his delightful slavery.
Affection rears a prison round, above
My thought, and on the boundless, trackless sea,
Thy bondsman still, I'd still be thrall to thee.

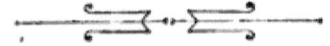

A dull grey dawn was followed by a heaven
Of faint blue tint, with pillowy clouds rolled high
Against the concave. Soon the sun, a mass
Of white and dazzling light was seen   Seen! No:
You look'd, and turn'd, and blinding shadows played
Before your eyes.   For he had stolen behind
Great steely belts of vapour; gave no sign
Save some few yellow-crimson touches near
The horizon pale, which proved no herald rays,
But legacies of his eclipsèd glory.
The clouds grew brighter, shone more pearly-white;
The horses stood but half awake, nor fed;
Lazily, languidly they switched their tails.
Up from the prairie rose the myriad songs
Of birds.   The bull-frog's plaintive note was heard
In pauses of the various melody.
The long legged night-hawk ran along the track
And uttered his harsh-grating cry.   The air
Was cool and balmy, odorous with scent
Of grass and flower   I sat me down to read.
My eyes I raised at intervals to watch
Put on a subtler polish the bright clouds.
Three Indians clad in cast-off clothes of whites,
All lank and dirty, listless, came and sat
A short way off.   Towards seven the sun grew hot
And made one long for branching bowery trees,
With their cool shadows and their murmuring leaves.

TRANSLATION OF GOETHE'S DER KOENIG IN THULE.

In Thule lived a noble king,
   All faithful to the grave;
Him, dying, his love –O, sacred thing!
   A golden beaker gave.

More prized than all his wealth beside,
   He drained it every meal;
Each time he quaffed its rosy tide,
   The tears began to steal.

And when death claimed him as his slave,
   His towns he reckoned up,
All to his heir he gladly gave,
   But not that golden cup.

A rich, right royal feast for all
   His faithful knights made he,
There in his high, ancestral hall,
   In his castle by the sea.

And there the aged toper rose;
   He drinks life's last glad glow,
And then the sacred cup he throws
   Into the waves below.

He sees it fall, fill, disappear
   Beneath the deep, deep sea,
Then closed his eyes without a tear,
   And no more a drop drank he.

YOUNG CANADA.

"The hulking young giant beyond St. Lawrence and the Lakes."
W. D. Howells in "Their Wedding Journey.

A youthful giant, golden-haired,
　　With fearless forehead, eye of blue,
And large and clear its frosty depths,
　　With fire within its darkn'ing hue.

His spear which dwarfs the tallest pine,
　　Is bound around with yellow grain,
His shield is rich in varied scenes,
　　To right and left loud roars the main.

A-top eternal snow is piled;
　　Bright chains of lakes flash down through woods
Now bleak, now green, now gold, now fire,
　　Touched by the season's changing moods.

He dreameth of unborn times;
　　With manhood's thoughts his mind is braced;
He'll teach the world a lesson yet,
　　And with the might'est must be placed.

Heaven's best star his footsteps guide !
　　Give him to know what's truly great !
Not wealth ill-got or ill-enjoyed;
　　For power- no thrall to lust or hate;

But equal heart—the thirst for truth—
  A mind strong to produce and pry—
The love of men—the generous heart
  That makes the hero glad to die!

If pure in purpose as he's strong,
  Nothing of danger need he fear;
But better far than base success,
  To ride on an untimely bier.

But fear be hushed! God's omens beckon;
  Who counselled wrong will soon be far.
Beyond the hill a voice is calling,
  Its notes ring clear above the jar

Of passing strifes and paling passions—
  Hell's wild battle 'mid mortal graves;
And with it, hark! the great bass mingles
  Of Atlantic and Pacific waves:

"Not Scotch, nor Irish, French, nor Saxon,
  But all of these and yet our own;
There are no beaten paths to greatness;
  Who'd scale those heights must climb alone.

Ierne's heart, compact of joy
  And sorrow, wealth of feeling brings;
France, sweetness for each word and act—
  The gaiety that ever sings.

From Scotland, thrift and strength you borrow
  John Knox's strength and Burns' liberal heart;
The Saxon breadth and compromise
  Shall lead; but you the larger part

Of your own destiny must be;
 Yours to direct—you light the fire—
The animating soul's your gift,
 For all fair things the high desire."

The voice dies o'er the dews of morning,
 Which round him glitter while shadows flee,
Bright concord beams from shore to shore,
 Glad union peals from sea to sea!

April, 1878.

FORWARD.

Who sneers she's but a colony—
  No national spirit there;
Race differences, faction's feuds
  Her flag to tatters tear?

What rises o'er those snowy plains?
  What flouts the Western sky?
Whence on the virgin white those stains?
  Whose is that crimson dye?

Rebellion's ensign blots the blue,
  And mars its fretwork gold,
And near those stains of crimson hue,
  Canadian hearts lie cold.

Another ensign! Trumpets ring!
  A youth this flag upholds;
And lo! from every side men spring
  And range beneath its folds.

Nor race, nor creed, the patriot's sword,
  Nor faction blunts to-day.
"Forward for Canada!" 's the word,
  And, eager for the fray,

Our youth press on and carpers shame,
  Their bearing bold and high,
For this young nation's peace and fame.
  Ready to do or die.

They come from hamlet and from **town**,
   From hill and wood and glade,
From where great palaces look down
   On streets that roar with trade;

From whence by floe and rocky bar,
   The Atlantic's held in check;
From where Wolfe's glory, like a **star**,
   Shines down on old Quebec;

From where Mount Royal rises proud
   O'er Cartier's city fair;
From where Chaudière with thundercloud,
   Flings high its smoke in air ;

From pleasant cities rich and old
   That gem Ontario's shore;
From where Niagara's awful plunge
   Makes its eternal roar ;

From each new town, just sprung to life,
   Mid flowery prairies wide;
From where first Riel kindled strife
   To Calgary's rapid tide

Upon the field, all rancour healed,
   There's no discordant hue;
The Orange marches with the Green,
   The Rouge beside the Bleu.

One purpose now fires every eye,
   Rebellion foul to slay,
" Forward for Canada !" 's the cry,
   And all are one to-day.

A SONG OF CANADA.

Columbia growls.
We care not, we,
We are young and strong and free.
The storm-defying oak's great sap
Swells in the twig.
A breath of power stirs round us from each sea,
And, big with future greatness,
Our hearts beat high and bold,
Like growing seas that smite the cliffs to dust.
You cannot make us blench,
The sons of freemen we, we must be free,
Heroic milk is white upon our gums
Where lion's teeth will grow;
You cannot make us fear;
With rythmic step we move on to the goal.

A nation's destiny is bright
        Within our eyes,
Deep-mirror'd in heroic will;
The future years like Banquo's issue pass:
        A crown is there,
No tinsel crown of Kings, no bauble;
        A people's sovereign will,
The crown of manhood in its noblest use,
Freedom, men worthy of her great reward.

Let the wolf growl,
The lion's whelp is undismayed.
A better part the child of Washington
Might play to-day—
To shun the jealousies, and shame the greed,
Which deluged earth with blood;
To reach a sister's hand,
To hold the faith which yet will rule,
That nations may be great and near,
    Live side by side, and yet
Keep adamantine muzzles on the beagles of the grave,
And with the glance of Justice strike
    Fell Slaughter dead.

Let the wolf howl.
Look to the West,
And note the giant's strides;
Then turn from feasts of hell,
From mumbling bones of faction,
And sweep back to obscure night,
The bat-like lives,
Whose wings are made in dark corruption's loom.
    Bestial mediocrities,
Whose eyes blear at the light,
And through the sacred edifice of our hopes,
Wherein they snugly build,
    Hold erring flight,
And mock the spirit of the mighty fane,
    And stain with ordure
The altar-cloth of Liberty.

O Canada! My country!
What is there thou might'st not do
If truth and honour guide thy steps?
Arise! To-day thy need is men!
Men full of all lore,
And master of this too,
Men of brain and heart and will,
Men who scorn base lucre's lures;
Men of such breed, where are they?
Factions which keep thy pocket lean,
     And torture fact,
And blind thine eyes to truth,
     Repress the wise.
But many a one true as the great of old
     Is thine.
Awake! Thou drowsing child of destiny!
Awake! Escape from clinging phantasms,
Soar free from shams and shibboleths,
To find thy kingly men—thy greatest need;
     Thy first of duties
To hear and hearken to the voice of truth.

Columbia, crying out like Rome
     And echoing Cato,
Touch with the present must forego,
Losing to-day she'll lose to-morrow too.
But thou— draw into all thy life
     The genius of the time;
Of Justice, Truth; Court Honour's smile;
Then mayest thou laugh at threats,
And win a happier, greater fate

Than owned the empires of the past,
    In palmiest days of power.
Awake! the dawn is tripping on the hills;
    The day's at hand;
I see a nation young, mature, and free,
    Step down the mountain side,
To take her proud place in the fields of time,
    And thou art she!

September, 1888.

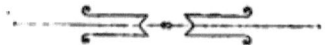